Witch'n

Joshua Braun

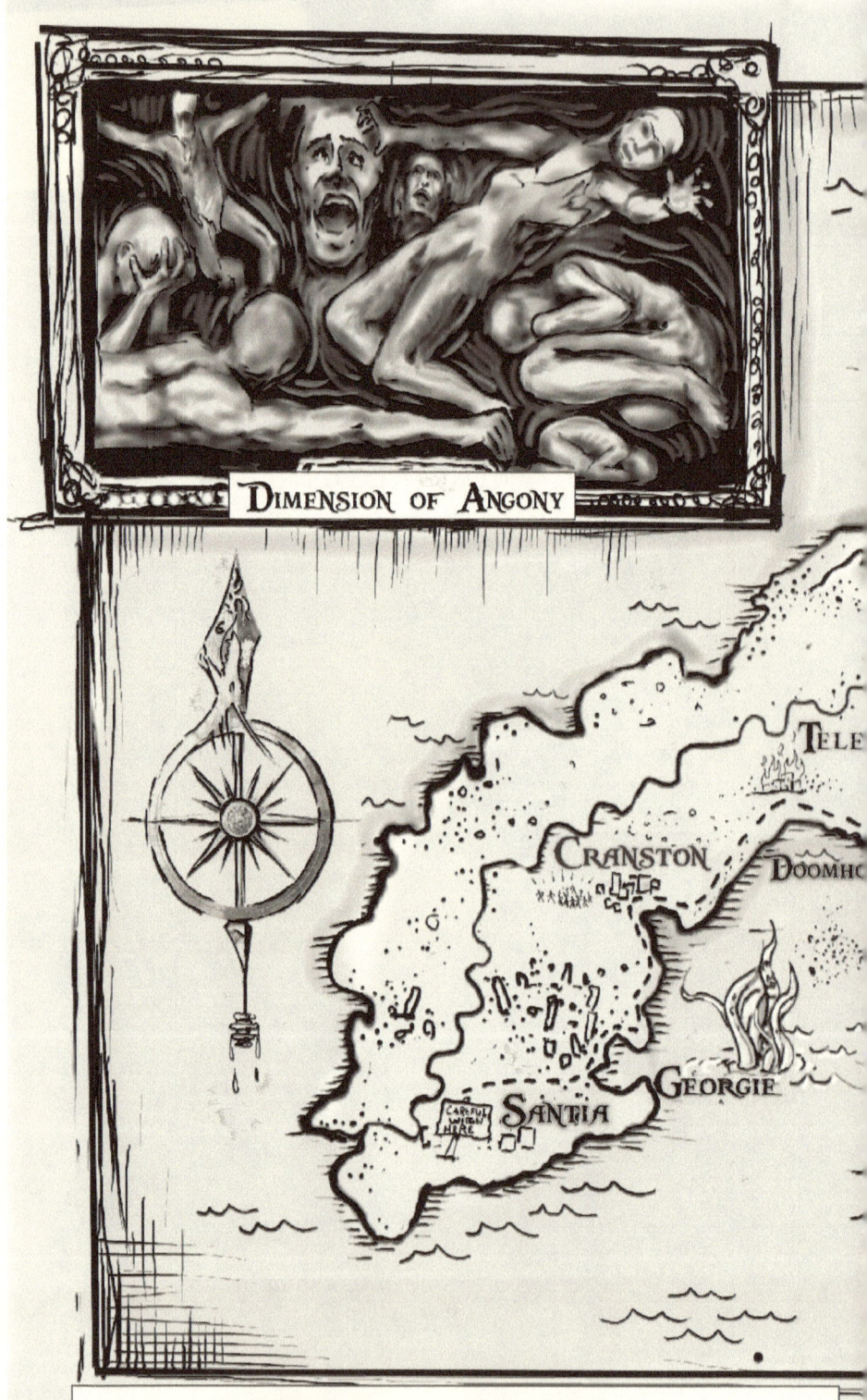

DIMENSION OF ANGONY

EMPATHODICY

Chapter 1

Blackened ruins were all that remained of the mighty kingdom Ernloheim. The land had been scourged of all life and turned to grey barrens. For miles no living thing stirred and a foul wind whipped up dust and ash as it howled across the land.

Ernloheim once led the last alliance against the forces of darkness, against the witch. In the end they had fallen, as all the cities of the world fell to her evil powers. Death lay scattered everywhere, the bones of heroes and monsters covering the earth, some still clutched the weapons that failed to save them in life.

Wicked magic blotted out the sun, fouled the land, and poisoned the rivers. An ever present cloud of blackness hung in the sky, never raining nor thundering, forever casting the land in a frozen eternal darkness. The whole of the world, called Cordemna, suffered the same curse, where green things no longer grew and the songs of birds fell silent. Overall not a great place to honeymoon.

A crystal palace had been erected where Ernloheim's shining castle had stood. It looked like a twisted hand clawing at all angles towards the sky. Thousands of pastel hues covered the facets of its warped fingers creating an ethereal aura which was the only light in the desolate land.

Inside of the palace the crystals did not glow. Torches provided light, each one reflecting a hundred times and lighting entire hallways. The soot could gather on the ceiling, but there was no shortage of slaves to clean it up.

One part of the palace saw no light at all most of the time, for as the palace stretched upward, it also plunged into the earth. In its deepest bowels was a cell built for a single man. He was Alteem, the last prince of Ernloheim. The man had fought till his legs could no longer stand and his arms could no longer raise his sword. His father had a spear plunged through his heart, his younger brother was stabbed a dozen times, his younger sister and mother had been beheaded in front of him. Alteem's eyes watched his entire kingdom leveled to the ground and all the world come to ruin. All he had ever known, or ever loved, was gone.

While the room existed in darkness most often, it was not without light now. A pale purple flame flickered in the witch's delicate hands. She rolled it over them idly as if it was a ball, her nails black, her skin so ghostly pale that in better light it was hard to see the features of her face. She was pretty, unnaturally so. The like that could drive people to madness to win her over. Maybe even to tear out their beating hearts from their own chest and offer it to her. It hadn't happened yet, but the witch was sure it could any day now.

Her hair had been like wildfire once, and still was in places, but the magics she so casually toyed with had turned it white at the roots and black at the tips, with strong highlights of green among its natural color. She was a small thing, for one who wielded such terrifying power, a couple of inches shy of five feet.

Pretty as she was, there was something unsettling about her face. The sort of thing a person couldn't quite put their finger on. If they stared long enough, and paid enough attention, they might notice her eyes did not quite match. They were both green, but one was slightly darker than the other. If you were close enough, as few ever were, you would see the patterns of the eyes were different. One looked like a starburst, while the other had three concentric circles.

She lounged in a satin couch, a blend of pink and purple. The witch ordered it dragged in after her visits to the cell became regular.

When Alteem had first been imprisoned they had tortured him once a week, dragging him out of the cell to be flogged while she watched and smiled. Then, she'd gotten bored of that, and left him rotting in the dungeon. More recently, however, she'd found a new way to torture him.

"I think it all started with my mother," she said. "Nothing was ever good enough for her." Her voice was lilting, with tremulous vowels.

"You had my mother executed in front of me," said Alteem.

"Could we not make this about you right now, I'm really having a tough time here."

Alteem said nothing, but stared blankly at the wall. The light from her flame reached just far enough to cast bars of shadow across his form.

"Where was I? Oh yes, my mother, horrid woman. It was one thing after another with her. 'Don't shake so much when you're sacrificing an animal to summon a demon,' it was my first time, surely I was allowed to be a bit a nervous. 'Shouldn't you be watching your figure?' 'You're supposed to smear blood left to right.' 'Don't play with your demonic minions.' 'Why don't you have a boyfriend?' I don't know mother, maybe because we live in a sentient swamp that opens up its thousand tooth maw to swallow anyone who doesn't know the secret paths. Maybe *that's* why I don't have a boyfriend, mother."

"Even when I killed her it wasn't good enough. I thought I'd do it out in the open, you know, the fair thing, give her a fighting chance, but no. 'Why aren't you killing me peacefully in my sleep? I guess you don't really love me. After all I've done for you,' No mother, I don't love you!"

The witch sat up in her couch. "Oh wow, I've never said that out loud before, if feels so good to finally admit it to someone. Talking to you always makes me feel better Alty, I'm so glad we started having these little chats."

"I loved my mother, she used to sing me to sleep when I was little," Alteem said, his body unmoving in the dark.

"My mother used to summon demons to invade my dreams and give me nightmares," she paused, not saying anything for a moment. "It wasn't supposed to be like this, you know, conquering the world. There was supposed to be parties, fun, parades. Everything the way I wanted it to be. I don't remember the last time I had fun, and I still don't have a boyfriend. I haven't had the time, what with running the world and such. It's nothing but work, work, work. I can't believe I'm saying this, but, I think I'm beginning to regret conquering the world and covering it in eternal darkness."

Alteem looked up from the wall to her, "You could always abdicate, give it all up."

The witch considered it. "Oh no I couldn't, imagine the embarrassment. Going to all that trouble and then just walking away. Raising an army of evil, marching it across the world, laying waste to my enemies, desecrating the land as we went, all for nothing, I'd never live it down. Then there's all the innocent people I've killed, am I just supposed to have let them die for nothing. How do you think I'd feel, knowing I'd killed them all, then just changed my mind after it was too late? It's just not fair."

"They already died in vain, trying to stop you."

The witch scoffed. "You're always so gloomy. You really should try and cheer up Alty. I know! How does double rations sound, hmmm? Two slices of bread? Bet that sounds pretty good."

Alteem went back to staring at the wall.

"There's just no pleasing you."

A knock came on the door. "This is supposed to be me time," the witch said, the hint of a threat on her voice.

"It's been an hour my dark Empress," Came a hoarse voice from the other side of the door. "It's almost time for you to hold audience in the throne room."

"Already?" The witch looked with pleading eyes up to the ceiling while sighing. "Fine, but this is exactly what I'm talking about. My life isn't my own anymore."

The witch got to her feet and walked towards the door, "I'll see you tomorrow Alty, you know, if you're still alive." The door opened, and her advisor Krekatin waited for her. It was a Holdorf, one of many beastly races she'd united in her conquest of the world. They had grey skin so tough it looked like leather, and milky eyes. No hair ever adorned their heads but black or white beards often grew on the chins of both men and women. The witch did not know if Krekatin was a man or woman, she had never cared to ask. The Holdorf appeared more diminutive than the other beastly races, matching the witches short height, but this was only due to the fact they hunched themselves over.

If there was one thing the Holdorf loved it was organizing things. They often didn't get very far when traveling since they'd frequently stop along the roads to organize pebbles or rocks. At the best of times they loved to organize parties, at the worst, armies. The witch had employed them for both of these talents. If there was one downside to their behavior, it's that they could be pretty catty about people's clothing choices.

In his rare free time, Krekatin could often be seen outside the palace organizing the bones outside. As a result, a radius of neatly aligned bones stretched out from the entrance.

Her guardsmen were comprised mostly of the wandering herds. They had no name for their own race, though humans called them Goatmen. They referred to themselves only by the name of their tribe and their rank within. This often confused the witch but she'd quickly found a way around it by referring to them simply as, "You there."

The heads of the Goatmen were, as one might expect, goat like. Upon their faces short muzzles protruded, covered in black fur. Dark crimson horns curled on the sides of their heads. They had feet but they were bestial, a cross between a wolf and man. They wore black plate mail and held long serrated halberds. A war-like people, they bickered with each other in blood feuds for thousands of years. The feuds stopped only long enough to raid villages and towns for supplies. They burned crops, caring nothing for agriculture, stealing livestock and people for their food. Only ash and destruction was left in their wake. It was all around agreed, however, that they were nice enough chaps once you got to know them.

The hallways of the crystal palace were much the same colors as its outside. They twisted and turned at random. Doors were mirrors that rippled and vanished when touched. There were no stairs, but passages ascended and descended at certain forks.

After traversing the mad labyrinth, Krekatin and the witch came to the throne room. She plopped down on her throne, a black metal claw forged in the fires of the flags and thrones of all those she had conquered. It had not been long in her rule, when she'd decided that the metal chair was "dreadfully uncomfortable" and added several throw pillows. This somewhat diminished its effect. Most recently, she'd added an ottoman.

Two columns of guards lined either side of the court hall. It sloped gently downwards towards the large opening at its end.

The witch sighed, then sighed again, then pouted. "Send them in," she said with a hand wave. A long line of peasants, clothed in rags and covered in dirt, approached the throne. "Wasn't there some talk about washing them before letting them into the palace?"

"We hadn't come to final a decision about that. You said you liked them to be reminded of how pitiful they were before you," said Krekatin.

"That does sound like me. Next time just wash them, I'm tired of the smell."

"Yes Empress."

"Step forward," the witch said, settling back into her pillows.

A woman stepped forward, stout and thick, but somehow still gaunt. Krekatin pounded a staff on the ground three time, "You are now addressing her Majesty, the Empress of all the Lands, Conqueror of the world, witch Supreme, Princess of Darkness, Master of all evil, Queen of Nations-"

"Skip it! Just, *skip* the introduction," the witch said. "What do you want peasant?"

"My name is Martha, and the people of my village are starving-"

"Ugh, this again," The witch rolled her eyes, "It never ends. Why are you people *always* starving?"

"Because you burned all our fields, blighted our livestock, and desecrated the land," said Martha.

The room grew still, the guards half flinching in preparation for what was to come. Everyone knew the danger of rousing the witch's wrath. She did not show mercy, she did not have patience, and she brooked no insolence.

"It was a rhetorical question," the witch said, her eyes narrowing.

Martha stepped forward, "Well it's true. It's your fault everyone's starving. If you're tired of the complaints then do something about it."

"How dare you speak to me like to me like that?" The witch got to her feet marched towards the woman, getting in her face. Well, she tried to, but the woman was a good half a foot taller than her and much wider. "I've killed people for less."

"Go ahead and kill me then, it's no worse than what you've already done."

"Maybe if you're village hadn't opposed me I wouldn't have desecrated your land."

"My village didn't oppose you, we surrendered immediately on the promise you'd spare us. You desecrated the land of ally and enemy alike."

The witch turned to Krekatin, "Did I?"

"Not all of them," said Krekatin.

"Hah," The witch turned back to Martha and pointed her finger with triumph, "not, **all** of them."

Martha put her hands on her hips and frowned at the witch.

"Okay fine," The witch twirled her hand and a decanter appeared with a purple liquid inside. "Take this is and sprinkle three drops, and only three drops, on your land. The desecration should clear up in about a week."

"What happens if I use more than three?" Asked Martha.

"Nothing, it's just wasteful. Now get out of here before I kill you or whatever." The witch returned to her throne and sat down. "Who's next?"

The woman left, her life intact, and everyone exchanging surprised glances.

A man stepped forward, his clothes brown rags dripping off of him. His skin was stretched thin across his bones. "My name is Taylor, the people of my village are starving."

The witch wailed, pounding her fists repeatedly on her throne. Then, she let out a whining moan as she sank deeper into her pillows, plopping her feet up on the ottoman. "Who's here about food?" The whole line of peasants raised their hands. "Fine then, I'll fix it, okay, if you all promise not to whine about it anymore."

The peasants nodded their heads with a few mutterings of "I promise."

"Fine, fine, FINE! I will remove the corruption from the land. Green things will grow again, rivers will run blue. The sun shall shine and birds sing once more. It will be spring again and all things shall be fertile and bear fruit. Bleh. Never mind how much of an inconvenience this is for me. It's not like anybody ever cared about how much work I had to do in order to corrupt the land in the first place. Who's next?"

"That was everybody," said Krekatin.

"Oh," said the witch. "So I have some free time?"

"There are several other things that could use your attention, your majesty."

The witch moaned, "Why didn't anyone tell me ruling the world would be so much work? And to think, I gave away that decanter for nothing now. Do you think I made it clear enough I wanted it back?"

Krekatin shrugged.

Chapter 2

The witch sat at the head of a large table. Representatives of all the factions who had sworn allegiance to her gathered around it. Her head was raised above all others. Given the size of some of the creatures present, this meant she needed a tall chair with a set of stairs leading up to it.

"The Bloodgash clan was clearly in violation of our raiding rights when they crossed the Hallish river," Said Oargut, leader of the one of the beastman tribes. Some said the beastman had come to this world from hell long ago. No two were exactly alike but they all seemed a cross between man and beast. Some had hooves for feet, others talons or clawed feet. Most were covered in a layer of fur and had yellow or red eyes. They might have horns, and most had hair, but others heads were decorated with feathers. Most unsettling of all, they each had one or two completely human features. Oargut had one hand that was human, but for the claws that ripped their way out his fingertips. One of his eyes was human, the other catlike.

The beastmen had been the first to join the witch's army. They respected power, and she had traveled among the mountains from clan to clan. Defeating their leaders one by one, it did not take long until the almost the entire species was under her command.

"Those warriors were only chasing after a group of slaves who'd crossed the river. They were perfectly within their rights to recapture them," Said Flamelash, a man who'd once been called the Bandit King. His eyes were red, and glowed slightly whenever shadows were cast upon his face. Many believed he had demon blood in him. He'd united the bandits and brought them into the witch's legions. Among those here, he was the only leader of any faction present.

"Stay out of this Flamelash," said Woodrot, Bloodgash's first bodyguard. "This is no business of landless bandits."

"I'll not be chastised by a filthy animal." Said Flamelash.

"How dare you?" said Oargut, pounding a fist into the table, the wood creaking beneath the force.

"It would be better if your kind were all chained up where you belong." Flamelash raised his eyes just enough to look at the beastman.

Woodrot leapt into the air, fists clenched. A streak of neon purple shot towards him. It engulfed Woodrot's body, flesh and bone melting away in an instant, leaving only dust behind.

"No fighting," said the witch, who was now looking at her nails. Everyone was staring at her. "What?" She said.

"Your Majesty," said Krekatin. "You did promise to stop killing people and just start restraining them."

"Did I? Oh, well I forgot, won't happen again. It might, actually, happen again, but I'll try harder to remember next time."

"Woodrot was my wife," said Oargut, his eyes looking with sorrow upon the pile of dust.

"I had no idea," said the witch. "Some of you are female?"

"How did you think we birthed more of us?"

"Ew, gross, I don't want to think about that. Oh no, now I'm thinking about it. I may vomit." The witch covered her mouth with one of her hands.

"Perhaps if you would do what you're supposed to and settled these matters we wouldn't resort to fighting," Ro'garod spoke, a Nestling, insect like creatures who looked like bipedal beetles. They stood five feet tall with three arms. Their eyes were far apart on their faces and they looked halfway between human and insect eyes.

The witch held up her free hand indicating she needed a moment, her other hand still trying to prevent her from vomiting. When she collected herself a couple of minutes later, she took a deep breath, and looked at Ro'garod. Wisps of blue lighting began to arc off of her hand.

"I'm sorry, your Majesty," said Ro'garod, throwing himself at her feet. "Please spare my life, I misspoke."

"You wish for me to settle things, do you? Very well then, since you can't play nice with your slaves, then no more slaves for anybody."

Protestations arose among the attending, all but Flamelash rising to their feet. The witch raised her hand again. Everyone fell silent.

"My decision on the matter is final. Slavery is here by ended across the world. Anyone caught with slaves will be executed."

"But, without slaves what are we to do?" Asked Oargut. "Since we conquered the world, all we have to do is enslave people, recapture escaped slaves, and steal slaves from each other. Sometimes we let slaves escape so we can capture them again out of sheer boredom."

"I don't know, try taking up knitting, I hear it's a soothing hobby. And if any of you are upset about this situation, you can take it up with, um," The witch looked at Krekatin.

"Ro'garod, your majesty," said Krekatin.

"Rogard," The witch stepped down from her chair and left the room, Krekatin following behind her. "What next?"

"Next is your, shall we say, appointment, with Alteem."

"Is it that time already? The days go so quickly yet seem so endless. If everything is prepared, I'll meet him there."

"Very good, your majesty."

The door to Alteem's cell was opened. Dust kicked off the ground. The guards unlocked the chains around his wrists and led him into the hallways of the palace. The light reflecting all along the hallway, stung his eyes. He was scrubbed down and shaved, but he did not know why.

Brought to another door, he looked to either of the goatmen for some indication as to what was happening. They gave none, and a moment later the door opened. Alteem gazed upon a sight he never thought to see again, the sky. He stepped through the door and tasted fresh air. It was fetid, and tainted with the corruption that had covered the world, but it was fresh. The door closed behind him.

"Look at it," said the witch. She reclined on a long chair on the balcony which looked out across the barren and broken land. Nothing stirred, there were few places left where anything did. "It's beautiful isn't it? My masterpiece, the death of the planet. Taking over the world was a mistake, overall, but it did have its moments. Conquering was so much more fun than ruling, and I was better at it. Sit."

There was a second chair next to the witch with food and drink. She herself had a cup in her hand. He was alone with her, perhaps if he was quick he could close his hands around her neck. Thin as she was, it would be a small thing to snap it. But then he already knew, she could not be killed by mortal means. His cousin had proven that in their last attack against her armies. Alteem led a head assault while Berrick snuck around with an elite force to try and assassinate her. Against the odds, it had worked, she did not even see as Berrick's sword swung at her neck. The blade rebounded in a flash of light, flying out of his hands. She had torn him apart a little at a time, using her magic to keep him alive. It had turned her attention away from the battle long enough for some to flee with their lives. Others had stayed to fight until the end. There had been nothing else left for them to do. "Why have you brought me here?" He asked her.

"I wanted to look at it one last time, and I didn't want to be alone. I couldn't think of anyone else," For a second the witch's eyes nearly had tears in them, but it quickly passed.

"Last time?" Alteem asked, looking back at the view.

"I'm removing the corruption from the land tomorrow. I cannot listen to another person whine about not having enough food. I could just kill everyone, but then I really would be all alone, instead of just feeling like I am."

"You've come to the wrong person if you want sympathy."

"Sit, eat, you used to be kind of handsome you know."

Alteem sat but he did not eat.

The witch took a sip from her cup. "It took a few days for the preparations. Much easier than casting the spell was since now I have an army of servants. I know you don't appreciate it, but this was a spell many had tried." She took a deep breath. "This was what paved the path of my conquest."

She was right, Alteem realized. Before her dark legion had descended from the mountains the land had turned sick. Crops had failed and the few that succeeded gave little yield. Everyone turned on each other, desperate for more farm land, but the land just grew sicker. Holy spells delayed the corruption. Nothing stopped it.

When the witch had showed up, the world was already half broken. If they had united at the start, they might have stopped it before it began. The beastmen had joined together before, and the surrounding kingdoms had come together to stop them, but the food shortage had turned them too much against each other. When the first kingdoms fell, evil creatures and men everywhere flocked to her banner. It took years of fighting to conquer the whole of the world, but it was too late by that time. Or perhaps there had been no hope at all against her magic. With a wave of her hand she could slay dozens and level buildings to the ground. Alteem took an apple from the table, no matter how sick the world got, the witch always seemed to have food. "Won't it take time for the world to heal?"

"I'm not some amateur magician foolish enough to think my magic comes from some imagined gods or spirits. I will cleanse the world with a single stroke. I mean yes, of course, things over all will take time to heal. A lot of people are dead, a lot of other things are dead. I scarred the land in some places, sunk a few islands, shattered part of a continent, carved some mountains to look like me. That's not something that just gets better. Overall though, it'll be fine." The witch smiled, it was that self-satisfied smile he'd seen so many times. It made him want to bash her head against the floor. It faded, and she looked sad again. "I don't want to rule the world anymore, I just don't know what else I'd do."

Alteem wanted to say something, but he didn't know what to say. For some, their innocence was the source of their goodness, but for the witch, innocence made her evil. She just didn't understand things. What place was there for a woman who had the power of a goddess but the wisdom of a petulant child?

"If I let you go Alty, what would you do?"

He thought about it, but could not come up with an answer. His family and friends were all dead, his home obliterated. The world he had known was gone and would never return. How could he start over with nothing but memories of everything lost. There was only one thing left for him to do. "I'd die."

"You're always so morbid," the witch sighed. "I don't know what I want Alty, but I don't want you to die."

"Keep me imprisoned then, and keep me alive." Alteem didn't really care anymore. He was dead already, it would just take time for his body to catch up.

"Give me your hand." He did not move. "Give me your hand or I will take it."

Alteem held out his hand and the witch took a knife from the table and cut open his palm. She then cut her own palm and clasped them together.

"Promise you will live, so long as you are able."

"Have you gone even crazier than usual?"

"Promise it!"

"Fine, I promise."

"Say the words, you will live so long as you are able."

"I promise I will live so long as I am able." Alteem felt something, he could not say what, like something in the distance closing around him.

"And I promise you your freedom, so long as it is mine to give. Goodbye, Alty, I did enjoy talking to you," She did not look at him as she left, but Alteem thought he saw her crying. She was a pitiable creature in her own right, but he could not pity her.

There was still food on the table, Alteem had little want of it, but he ate some, and took more that would not perish quickly. The door was open, and he walked through. The guards stood there, and he expected them to put him in chains again, but they did not move. Alteem took a few steps away from them. They remained still, so the former prince began to wander the halls.

He'd spent the last many years in the crystal palace, how many he did not know, but he'd never actually been around in it before. Its pathways twisted, and bent, and curved around. The magic of the palace even caused things to change from time to time. Sometimes he'd be walking and look out a window only to realize he was walking upside down. If the witch really meant to free him, it would have been nice if she'd have told him how to leave.

Stopping a moment to sit and eat, memories crept upon his mind. In the darkness memories were all he'd had. Now he was free, it remained just as true, but in the light it was harder to see them. He could not see the faces that no longer were. Perhaps he'd spent too long in the dark, for he found he missed it. Maybe it was just the nature of humans to miss the familiar, even if it is more horrible than change.

After finishing food he resumed his wandering. Days could pass and all he would see were empty rooms, which led to hallways, which led to rooms. Other times he found many others, servants who had not long ago been slaves. Food could always be found, abandoned on plates or in storerooms. From time to time he met fellow wanderers who were just as lost as him. One man insisted that the palace was all there was, and that the outside world was nothing but a false dream.

As the days wore on the boredom got to him. He tried marking walls to keep track where he'd been, but people kept washing off his marks. Once he thought he was near the bottom from looking out the windows, but an hour later he was near the top. He did get to watch as the black clouds left the sky and sun shown for the first time since the witch had cast her spell. All those years trapped in the cell, he'd never dreamed he'd see the sun again. Yet standing next to the window he could feel its warmth on his face. He thought he might cry, but he'd long ago run dry of tears.

A day came when he stumbled into the throne room while the witch was holding audience. An older woman with a large hearty body was standing before the witch.

"No, no," said the witch. "You promised, no more complaining about food."

"We're not complaining about the food," Said the woman. "It's transporting the food that's the problem. We grow the grain, we need to then transport the grain to a mills, silos, and of course, granaries."

"Well what do you want me to do about it?"

"We need roads."

"No, you have roads, I've seen them."

"Yes, but roads need maintenance."

"What!?" The witch moaned and slumped down into her throne, throwing one of her legs over the side. "Why is everything so much work? You know what doesn't have to work, trees. I should make every-one a tree."

"Trees?" The woman tilted her head up and gave the witch a queer look.

"Think about it, they don't have to do anything, it all just happens for them. They just get to relax all day, basking in the sun. It must be nice to be a tree."

"Don't bugs burrow under the bark of trees?"

"Ew, you're right," The witch shivered. "That's like their skin. Being a tree sucks. I killed a man by having bugs burrow under his skin once. I really regretted it, not the killing part, but watching it happen. Some images stay with you."

"Roads." The woman insisted again.

The witch paused, frowning at the woman. "Fine, I'll look into this whole 'roads' thing. Now go away."

The woman left the room. Seeing it empty except for the witch and her minions, Alteem stepped inside. The witch saw him. Her face lit up and she got up from her chair and ran towards him. "Alty, you came back." She sounded on the verge of tears.

"I never left," Alteem said.

"You couldn't leave me?"

"Yes," he said. "Literally, I can't find my way out of this place."

"Oh," her smile faded and her shoulders slumped as her run to-wards him came to a stop a couple of feet away. "I'll show you out." The witch led him through twisting corridors of the Crystal Palace. "Really, I regret making this place so complicated. I wanted to show off, but every now and then someone gets completely lost and we don't find them until their corpse begins to smell. I probably should have consulted an architect or something. Except I think I killed most of them." She burst into laughter. "I killed most of everybody, didn't I? Ahhhh, those were the good old days. Here we are then." They stopped at a door. There was nothing special about it. It looked like any other door in the palace. "We already did the emotional goodbye thing so..." She stopped talking, her mouth hanging open for a few seconds. Then she shrugged and walked away.

Alteem touched the door and it rippled away, outside was green grass and sunshine. He stepped through, and breathed the clean air. He was free again, something he'd never thought to dream he might be. What was he to do? Everything he'd known was gone. His home and his people had been destroyed, his family killed. He had nothing. There was only one logical thing left to do with his life. Alteem set out on the road for what he believed to be the final quest of his life, to become a drunk.

Chapter 3

The goal of becoming a drunk was all well and good, but it did require drink, and drink required money. If Alteem had been thinking, he might have asked the witch for money, but the opportunity had passed. Given the recent destruction of the world, he doubted begging would get him very far.

As he walked down the road, plants growing inbetween its cracks, he considered his skills. Having been raised a prince he was mostly skilled in statecraft, politics, diplomacy, and war. These were all good skills for a ruler to have. No longer being a ruler, he wasn't sure in what way he might apply said skills. It might have been possible for him to find work as an officer in an army or a diplomat somewhere. This too was impossible, since there was only one government and army left in the world. He had no interest in working for them.

As a young lad he'd been forced to memorize the heraldry of every noble house in his and neighboring kingdoms, but they were all dead now.

He was a fine hunter with a bow, but without, which he was, he could do little. He'd learned a little in the art of singing, but not nearly enough to earn any wages as one. He also had some notion of fashion, but again, this was not of much use given his current circumstances. Being a prince, as it turned out, was really only useful if you in fact were, a prince.

Perhaps he was going about this all wrong. It was not as if he needed a great deal of money, he simply needed enough money to be in a constant state of intoxication. There was always need for un-skilled labor somewhere. There had been before the end of the world anyway.

The first thing he needed to find was a town where people lived. Given the severely diminished population it proved to be a difficult task. The first town he found was completely empty, the buildings burnt to ruin. As he walked among the blackened wood, he remem-bered the place, of course he did, these had been his lands. Alteem had been numb with sorrow for many years, but being in this place he felt the invisible hand of pain clutch at his heart. Every street held the shadows of the people who had once lived here. Their prince had failed them, and now they were dead. The witch had once enslaved people from all over, but of Ernloheim she'd left none living, save himself.

The ghosts in his mind stared at him, judging, pleading, dying. Though he'd not been here when the place was destroyed, he could still hear the screams. Not just their screams, but the screams of a war fought for years, the faces of thousands dead, of the witches snarling hordes as they fought. He wanted to turn and run away, but he could not leave. The more he walked through the town the more the pain he had buried deep came crawling back to him.

How many might have lived here, how many were dead. He felt them, clawing at him from the grave. His people, his family, their pains becoming his pain, making his body tremble as they pulled him through the streets to witness his failure.

It was all gone, and it was his fault. A piece of sharp wood jutted up from the ruins.

Alteem felt himself pulled towards it. Gripping it in his hands, and the hands of the dead, he placed the tip over his heart. Then, he thrust himself forward, but didn't. Something stopped him, but it was not his own mind. For a moment he thought the ghosts of the past really had come back, unwilling to let it end, but then he remembered the promise he'd made to the witch. She'd bound them both in magic. Her last cruelty to him had been to suffer him to live.

Rain began to fall, and Alteem collapsed backwards into the mud. He lay there, letting the rain fill in for the tears he could no longer make, defeated again.

The sky turned dark as he lay there, and eventually sleep took him. He awoke the next day to a bright dawn, and a sound disappeared from the world with green growing things. A bird perched on the same jutting wood he'd tried to kill himself with. It sang, a sound all the more beautiful for he'd thought to never hear it again.

With some difficulty, he pulled himself out of the mud, puddles of rain gathered around him on the streets. Much of the ash and dust had washed away and the earth was brown again. He even thought he saw the start of some patches of grass.

'Very well,' He told himself. 'If I must live then I shall live.' He resumed his journey, knowing only that he was moving away from the palace, from Ernloheim, avoiding any buildings. His diet consisted of grubs, berries, and nuts he managed to find. Eventually he came to a river and followed it. Not bothering to keep track of the days, he just kept moving. The sun rose, and the sun fell, and the last prince of Ernloheim moved one foot in front of the other.

Towns started to have people, but he still avoided them. He kept away from others as he traveled. Living as such might have turned a man wild and feral looking, but his time in the prison had already done that. As it were, getting covered with dirt only improved his appearance. His skin grew healthier under the sun, and traveling let his muscles regain lost strength.

He journeyed for what must have been nearly a year, wandering, walking, avoiding voices in the distance. A day came when he decided to bath in the river he'd been following for so long. The water was near ice cold, but he didn't mind. As with so many things, he'd not bathed in so very long. He washed the stink off of himself, but could do little about his clothes, save let them soak awhile.

After, Alteem returned to his wandering. He found a road and followed it until he heard sounds. The sort of sounds he had not heard in many years or ever thought to hear again. Given the fact that he'd been experiencing a lot of these sorts of things since getting out of prison, it was starting to feel a lot less special. A person can only experience so many things they haven't experienced in years and never thought they'd experience again before the novelty wears off.

He heard the sound of celebration. Alteem nearly turned away, but it was curiosity made him remain. What could people possibly be celebrating given all the terrible things that had befallen the world?

The people had dark skin with colorful clothes. Westerners, Alteem knew, peninsula dwellers. He had not realized he had travelled so far.

They had colorful ribbons strung up all around the town, with more ribbons hanging down from them. Their houses were made of a rust colored stone. They had their rice dishes displayed across their thin bread topped with meat, spices, and vegetables.

Alteem had never much cared for the peninsula's spicy food, but he had only eaten bugs and berries for the past year. He approached, slowly. Everyone was so caught up in the celebration he had to get quite close for anyone to notice him.

It happed all at once. The music stopped, the dancing stopped, the drinking stopped, and everyone turned to look at the wildman who had wandered up to their village.

"Pardon me," he said, speaking slowly for he had not spoken to a person in a long time. "I was wondering, what are you celebrating?"

A man stepped forward, at least a head taller than Alteem and twice as wide. "You look like you just got out of hell."

"Yeah," Alteem said. "Or perhaps I'm still there and I went mad. This may be just a dream. The world is nearly dead, it seems mad enough people might be celebrating."

"This is no dream, yeah, and you must have been in hell for a very long time. The world celebrates the anniversary of the abolition of slavery. It has been one year since the witch declared all slaves be free. I'm told people did not believe it when the posters went up declaring it. But then we started to come back, all at once."

"We?"

The man let out a laugh that carried across the crowd. "I was good stock, yeah." He pounded his chest. "But now I am a man again, a free man, stock no more. Come, sit at our table, yeah. You look like you could use some good food."

The man brought Alteem to a table. A woman with hints of grey in her black hair sat there. She might have been close to Alteem's age. A young boy sat there as well, near manhood.

The large man sat down. "My name is Mateo, this is my older sister Alma, and her son Mathew. What is your name stranger?"

"Al-" Alteem paused, people knew his name. He was not a prince anymore, just another man. "Allard."

Mateo put a plate of food in front of him. "Where do you come from friend?"

"Ernloheim."

Everyone around the table froze and no one spoke as Alteem started to eat off his plate. It was Alma who broke the silence, "I didn't know anyone from Ernloheim still lived. We'd heard the whole kingdom had been wiped out."

"Nearly," said Alteem. "As far as I know I am the last."

Mathew spoke, "You're not the last. Some people say the last Prince of Ernloheim still lives and that one day he'll return and free us from the witch."

"That's just fools talking," said Mateo. "If he had the power to stop the witch he would have done it before she destroyed everything."

"Yeah," said Alteem. "The last Prince of Ernloheim can't help anybody anymore."

Mathew bowed his head in disappointment.

"You shouldn't squash the boy's hope," said Alma. "There's been little enough of it these past years, and it is a day for hope."

"No sense hoping for things that will never happen," said Mateo. "The witch will rule forever. Better hope she becomes kinder. She ended slavery, maybe she's changing."

"She isn't changing," said Alteem. "She's just bored of things the way they are."

"And how would you know?"

"Just a guess," Alteem reached for a drink, brought it to his lips, but could not swallow.

Mateo laughed, "Too strong for you, yeah?"

Alteem looked at the drink, puzzled as to what was stopping him. Then he remembered the last magic the witch had performed on him. He had to live, and alcohol was technically poison. "It's been so long, I forgot. I was cursed to be unable to drink alcohol."

"That's rough, yeah."

Alteem stared at the drink. "I can't drink it, but someone could force it down."

"What are you thinking?"

"I'm thinking I need help."

Mateo stood up and addressed everyone, "Our new friend here has been cursed to abstain from drink. But he has requested we help him keep it down. Who wants to help him get drunk, yeah?"

A cheer arose up from many people as they held Alteem down and forced liquor down his gullet. It was a team effort, but Alteem finally managed to succeed in his quest to be drunk.

Chapter 4

Alteem started a new life as Allard. With the reduced population there was plenty of work to be had. He'd work, collect his pay, then it was to the tavern with Mateo to get drunk. It became quite a game of the town to try and think of new and better ways to help Allard drink.

He stayed with Mateo and his family, helping with rent, food, and other jobs around their small home, just out of sight of the rest of town. Alma didn't think him a good influence on Mateo or Mathew, and she was probably right. The world began to return to normal. The roads were rebuilt, a school went up, then a hospital. They heard a university was founded in a city not far away. Mathew began to study to go there. Alteem helped out with the things he'd learned of philosophy, science, and math as a prince.

When asked he said he'd been a scholar before the fall of the world. Eventually more parents paid him to tutor their kids and soon he became a teacher at the school. He started drinking less since he needed to remember things he'd learned long ago. The world was healing, and impossibly, so was he.

He doubted he could ever completely recover from what had happened, but he had a sort of life again. Never had he thought he'd be able to get that much.

The fifth anniversary of the end of slavery arrived. Mathew was to go to university soon, along with four other children from the town.

26

The celebration doubled as a sendoff for them. Alteem, in the interest of keeping some dignity as their teacher, elected not to be strapped down and force fed alcohol.

Everyone was dancing when they came marching in, twelve Beastmen armed with axes poles and spears. The celebration stopped as everyone shied away from the Beastmen.

Mateo stepped forward. "What are you doing here?"

"We're here for our slaves," said one of the Beastmen.

"No more slaves," said Mateo.

The Beastmen spat, "We don't care what the witch says anymore. We're tired of building roads, schools, and hospitals. We're raiders not workers. We get others to do the work for us. Now surrender some of your folk and we'll leave you unharmed."

"The witch said the penalty for slavery is death, I don't think you want that, yeah. Move along, and we'll forget about this."

"Won't be our death," The Beastman lunged at Mateo. The huge man managed to grab one by the horns and smashed its head into a table. The creatures skull caved and its sword clattered to the ground. Several spears pierced Mateo. Screams emanated from the crowd and Alteem ran forward.

Mateo lay on the ground bleeding and Alteem was at his side.

"You want to die too, or will you hand them over?" asked the Beastman.

Mateo reached up and pulled Alteem close, "Don't let them take them, Alteem." Then his arms fell back to the ground.

He had known who I was the whole time, Alteem thought.

"I asked you a question human."

Alteem had lost another friend. Had he not lost enough that the world was still taking from him.

"Hey human," A Beastman jabbed a spear at Alteem. Alteem caught it with his hand. The Beastman tried to pull it back but Alteem ripped it away. He felt his other hand grab the sword that had fallen and he spun to his feet and slashed the Beastman's throat. The creature fell to the ground and the other Beastman pulled back in surprise.

Alteem took advantage of the moment and lunged. He plunged the spear through the chest of one, and slashed another across its belly. His sword came round and sliced off a chunk of skull from another as he felt a spear pierce his side. He stabbed the one who speared him and just managed to pull back as a sword cut a gash in his cheek. He cut down two more, but felt something stab into his leg and shoulder. He spun round, beheading one and then stabbing another.

He moved to take the two others but they threw down their weapons and ran. He sank to his knees, dimly aware of the world. Alma was before him, "Who are you really?" she asked.

"I am Alteem, last Prince of Ernloheim," Then he passed out from his wounds.

Alteem woke up to the sounds of conversation. It was Mathew and Alma.

"I'm not leaving you here alone," Mathew said.

"I'll be fine," said Alma. "Once Allard...Alteem wakes up he'll be able to help me out."

Alteem's head hurt, he must have hit it when he fell. His cheek burned, as did his leg and side where he'd been stabbed. Struggling to his feet, he managed to reach the door.

"What if, what if he doesn't wake up?"

"I'm tougher than that Mathew," Alteem said. Both Alma and Mathew turned to look at him.

"Are you really him?" Mathew asked.

"Not anymore," said Alteem.

"But you could stop the witch, rally the people against her."

"There is no stopping the witch, I saw it myself. She cannot be killed by mortal means."

"She sent those Beastmen here, they killed Mateo."

"No she didn't," Alteem took a seat, he was still low on blood and standing was taking its toll. "You heard the Beastmen, they came here against her orders. If you really want to take care of your mother, go to university. Get an education and all that goes with it. That's the best way you can take care of her. I'll do what I can in the meantime."

"And who's going to look after you old man, you can barely stand." Mathew leaned against the wall. Alma moved over to Alteem to look at his bandages.

"Don't forget why I can barely stand. In my prime I could have killed twenty of the things and not taken a scratch."

"Liar."

"I did have armor then." Alteem smiled for a moment, then his face grew sad as he remembered a time when he'd been prince.

"Alright, I'll go." Mathew said, grabbing his travelling bag. "You'd better keep your promise to take care of her, I know she'll do a better job taking care of you." He hugged and kissed his mother, shook Alteem's hand, and walked out the door.

Alteem's life resumed, but it was lonelier without Mateo. He missed him, as did Alma. They sought solace in each other. It wasn't the sort of love that people wrote stories about, but they did love each other. They had both lost much, as had everyone, and love did not come easy in the world anymore.

The years continued on, Alteem and Alma married, and Mathew came home for a short visit talking about some new pamphlet. A man named Sergei Haffleford had written a manifesto against the witch. It said many things, among them that consent must come from the will of the governed. Whoever the man was, Alteem did not think he would live long after upsetting the witch.

A couple more years passed, and Mathew returned home. He opened up a private law practice in town and did quite well for himself. The man who'd written the pamphlet still lived, much to everyone's surprise and rumors began to circulate the witch was dead. Alteem knew they weren't true, but she certainly wasn't the witch she used to be.

Alteem was closing up the schoolhouse one day. He took a moment to reflect on his life, how it'd become something good again. Perhaps, after everything, there was hope for the world. He exited locking the door behind him. Then he heard people behind him shout and scream. He turned around and people were fleeing. A few at first, but as the panic spread, more and more fled, dropping whatever they were holding.

He sought what they were staring at, fearing more Beastmen had come, cursing himself for not keeping the sword. Then, when he saw it, he knew it could only have been her. Only she inspired that sort of terror in people.

"Hello Alty," The witch said, a wicked smile spreading across her face. "So good to see you again."

Chapter 5

It had been nearly a decade since he last saw her, and she looked exactly the same, beautiful, pale, and with a cruel smile hidden just behind her eyes. He froze, hoping it was a nightmare. He had a life, had she come to destroy it all over again.

"Aren't you going to say hello, it has been so long since we last saw each other." She didn't even look at him as she spoke.

"What are you doing here?" He snarled at her.

"Wow, I forgot how rude you were."

Alteem marched over to her and tried to grab her by the arm. He pulled back as a shooting pain shot up his arms.

"Come Alteem you know better than to try and hurt me."

"Inside," He pointed to the school.

She crossed her arms and stared up at him.

Alteem sighed, "Inside, please."

"Don't we feel better? A little politeness goes a long way." The witch marched into the school, opening the door with a wave of her hand.

Alteem followed behind her, closing the door and locking it. "What are you doing here?"

"Is this what you do now, are you a teacher?"

"Yes."

"Well I hope you teach your students to be more polite than you are. I always wondered what it would be like to attend a normal school." Her eyes lit up as an idea came to her. She plopped down on one the desks. "Teach me a lesson."

Alteem just stared at her.

"Oh, come on, it'll be fun."

There were a great many lessons the witch needed to learn. Most of which would have been better taught at the point of a sword. He picked up a chalk and began writing on the board. "Ethics and morality," he began. "How we treat each other, and the consequences of those actions-"

"I was wrong this is boring," The witch began to idly kick at the desk in front of her.

"Then why don't you tell me why you're here?"

"Maybe it would be better if we had some other kids in the classroom. Make it more authentic."

"I am not going to force a bunch of children to sit in a classroom with you."

"Oh you're probably right," The witch slumped in her desk. "Children are always terrified of me. I don't know why?"

"Maybe because you destroyed the entire world and forced it into servitude under you."

"I know, but look at me, I'm so pretty. How could a kid be afraid of this face?" The witch sat back up in her desk and struck a pose.

"It doesn't matter how good looking you are on the outside, if you're hideous on the inside."

The witch suddenly looked terrified, an expression he had not seen before on her face. "Is that true, oh no, that's not good at all. It does explain a lot, come to think of it." The witch went silent as she became lost in thought. She snapped out of it slapping the desk, "That settles it, I'm swearing off evil."

"What?"

"No more evil, I'm becoming good. Nothing good ever came from being evil anyway." She snapped her finger. "Which makes sense because why would anything good ever come from evil, because it's evil. You're a good teacher Alty."

Alteem was now certain he had to be dreaming.

"It's actually good that you make such a great teacher because you were a lousy prince. Look what happened you're kingdom."

"Why are you here!?"

The witch crossed her arms and pouted. "They deposed me."

"Deposed?"

"Yes."

"You?"

"Yes."

Alteem could not believe he was going to ask it but, "Why didn't you just kill them all?"

"Well I was going to but then I thought, this is my chance to get out. I hated ruling the world and this was the perfect excuse."

"Why did they do it?"

"Something about consent of the governed and a constitution, I don't know, I wasn't really listening. I should have never let them start attending university."

"The monsters started to attend university."

"All the humans were going, and so they wanted to go, and they started whining, and I am just so sick of people whining at me."

"Maybe you should start from the beginning."

"Can we do it over dinner, I'm getting hungry?"

Alteem thought carefully about it. He could think of nothing worse than exposing his new family to this creature, but he couldn't take her some place public. What choice did he have?

Alma set down a plate for each of them. Her and Mathew had not stopped staring at the witch since Alteem had brought her home.

"What did you say this was called?" The witch asked poking at her plate.

"A burrito," Alma said. Not touching her own food.

"The thing is, I'm a vegan, for my skin-"

"Eat it," said Alteem.

The witch lifted the burrito to her face, took a small nibble off of it, then put it down.

"Start from the beginning, what happened?" Alteem asked.

"As you know," Began the witch. "I lifted my corruption from the world because I was tired of everyone complaining about food. Then, you saw, they wanted roads, but as it turns out there are a lot of roads. I get around flying on a broom so I wasn't aware, but they're every-where. Only a few people remained alive who knew how to build roads, so we had to start educating people again. We started to build schools and universities. Of course, academia requires a strong eco-nomic infrastructure to support it so we needed to strengthen the middle class. So, we started to draft discrimination laws to make sure everyone had equal opportunity to work as well as a welfare program for those out of work or unable to work."

"You...started a welfare program."

"Yeah, of course, you need a strong welfare estate to prevent people from falling into a cycle of poverty. That's just obvious, you must have been a terrible prince, so, anyway. There were some concerns over the new global economy. What was to stop people from exploiting poorer workers in other parts of the world for cheap labor? After all no more slavery so people were going to try and get cheap labor somehow."

"Why *did* you end slavery?" Alteem asked, suddenly curious.

"Oh, who remembers?" The witch said waving her hand. "We de-cided to institute a global minimum wage as well as global working standards to prevent people from exploiting poor populations. Some places are richer than others, and wanted a higher minimum wage so we allowed them to set a higher wage, but no one could go below the minimum wage."

"What about businesses that couldn't afford to pay employees the minimum wage?"

"We gave them tax deductions, and in the case of essential businesses to a community we instituted grants and subsidies."

"Surely people must have opposed some of this."

"Not really, I killed off most of the aristocracy and wealthy people to prevent anyone from challenging my power when I first conquered the world. With them out of the way making the world a better place was smooth sailing. Anyway, once everyone started getting an education suddenly they all wanted rights. Can you believe it? No appreciation for anything I'd done. Here I'm thinking, the whole reason I did all of this was so people would stop complaining, but it was always something. Medical research, scientific advancement, deforestation, which is actually a big problem, I looked into it and we're running out of trees. Granted, some of it is my fault, I did poison most of the world and made it nearly impossible for anything to grow, but you people are so irresponsible when it comes to this sort of thing. Still, one of my minions discovered this new thing, coal, very promising."

"How did you end up here?"

"Like I was saying, everyone wanted rights now. I knew this would happen too, once I started letting people have their way they just wanted more, more, more. So this council, I started a council with elected officials from all the different factions I rule. They approach me and they don't want me to rule anymore. As I said, at first I was going to kill them all, but then it dawned on me I could finally get out of ruling the world without embarrassing myself."

"Again, why are you here, specifically?"

"Well if I'm not ruling the world I'm not just going to sit by and let someone else do it, especially after I did all the hard work of conquering it. I thought I'd start a rebellion to overthrow whoever takes my place, but then I realized no one's going to rally behind me. I need someone people like, a hero, and who do I know that just happens to be good at rallying people?"

Alteem leaned forward over the table. "To make sure I understand this, you want me to help you start a rebellion to overthrow your own government?"

"Exactly, do you want to leave now or get a good night's sleep first?"

"Forget it."

"Oh, come on, it'll be fun. Like an adventure. I've never had an adventure before. Lots of people went on adventures to kill me, but I've never had my own."

"I'm not going to help you cut another bloody path through a world that has finally begun to heal from the last time you went to war."

"But I'm good now, remember, I decided."

"You are not good now!" Alteem slammed his fist into the table. "You cannot just decide to be good. It's not about what you think you are, it's how you treat others. You can't simply erase the decades of slaughter and torture. You have wiped entire peoples away. I don't know if there's even anything good in you."

"Okay, hurtful, but you're right, I don't know how to be good. I mean literally, no one taught me how. That's why I need you Alty."

"Here's your lesson on how to be good, don't start a war just because you don't want someone else to be in charge."

"Are you sure?"

"Yes."

Mathew spoke, "But there is a good reason for rebellion."

"I knew it," the witch said clapping.

"Shut up," Alteem said to the witch and she slunk into her chair pouting. "What do mean Mathew?"

"The witch is a tyrant-" Mathew said before being interrupted by the witch.

"Was a tyrant."

"The witch, WAS, a tyrant. We cannot simply let some other despot sit in her throne. This is the first real chance we've had at freedom. And we can make it a real freedom this time. No more kings and emperors. A government for the people, and of the people."

"He seems smart, I think we should listen to him," said the witch.

"I know what she did to you Alteem," Mathew continued. "But all the stories called you a hero. This is a chance to make the world a better place. If the witch is on our side this time, we'll be unbeatable."

Mathew was right, Alteem knew. When had the boy gotten so smart? He looked at Alma, she seemed hopeful at the chance for a better world, but sad that he would have to go. Then he looked at the witch, she had a hopeful look as well. Like a child hoping someone will give her candy. Had he not given enough to the world? He had a life again, must he now lose it because of this creature? "You took my world away from me once witch. You killed everyone I cared about and tortured me for years. You owe me an honest answer to this question. Do you sincerely wish to renounce your evil ways?"

The witch drew back from him, her face falling. For the first time since he'd ever known her, there was a glimmer of a human being in her eyes. Then it was gone. "Of course, Alty, I said so didn't I?"

"What will you do once it's all over?"

"Settle down I think, start a family."

"You really think anyone will want to start a family with you?"

"I'll just find someone shallow, so they won't care about my personality."

"Is it strange that I want to hug her and strangle her at the same time?" Alma asked.

"No that's normal for her," said Alteem.

"Oh, you can't strangle me, I have magic that protects me. No one's ever tried to hug me before, so I don't know what happens if people do that."

"There it is again," said Alma.

"What is your plan?" asked Alteem.

"First," said the witch. "I was thinking I would summon a demon."

"Summoning a demon is evil."

"No, well maybe a little, but hear me out. I'm not going to use the demon to cause any harm. I figure we stage a big fight between you and the demon. Really establish you as a hero people can rally behind again."

"Deceiving people into following you is also evil."

"Is it? I mean, we're not harming anybody. All it takes to summon a demon is to sacrifice one little baby and-"

"Stop, sacrificing a baby is definitely evil."

The witch paused, confusion on her face, then she smiled. "You're kidding with this one right? Right? Right?" She looked around the room looking for confirmation but did not find it. "Really?"

"How can you not know that killing a baby is evil?" Alteem asked.

"Babies are the worst. I mean **the worst**. What's so evil about killing one?"

"Because they're babies."

"But that's my whole point. If you call someone a baby it's not a compliment, it's because babies are awful. They make messes and don't clean up after themselves. They don't appreciate anything you do for them. They don't communicate what's wrong with them in a healthy manner, they just whine until someone fixes it for them. They do nothing for themselves. They just consume resources and contribute nothing to society. And they shit themselves, Alteem. They shit themselves and everyone else has to clean it up."

"They're babies."

"But there's tons of them. It's not like we can't always get more. Really, in the demon summoning world they're the ultimate renewable resource. Also, and I'm being honest here, if there's anything conquering the world has taught me, there's a lot of people making babies who really shouldn't be. Plus, who would bring a child into the world the way it is. It's a mercy killing if you think about."

"You're the one who made the world this way."

"I'll concede that, but my point still stands."

Alteem rubbed his temples. He had never thought before that he would have to debate the morality of murdering a baby, or that he would be losing the debate. "You're just going to have to take my word for it, murdering a baby is one of the most evil things you can do."

"Fine, no baby murder, for now, but I want to revisit this later because I'm still not convinced."

"Do you have a non-baby murder plan?"

"Not really, baby murder is usually my reliable go to."

"Well, you're right, NOT about the baby murder. It is going to be hard to get people to rally together."

"Maybe not as hard as you think," said Mathew. "I know your generation was broken, but mine is ready to fight. They just need a reason to think they can win."

"Like the witch switching sides," said Alteem. "The difficulty will be in convincing people she really has."

"I really have," said the witch. "We'll just tell them."

"Your reputation is not one of honesty."

"I never lied."

"You constantly lied."

"Not on purpose, I just sometimes forget my promises. That's not lying"

"That's another lesson for you, remembering a promise is an important part of keeping it."

"Ugh, being good is hard."

"It's been less than an hour."

"What? It has to have been longer than that." The witch glanced out the window to check the position of the sun.

"It can't be done. I don't even think you can be good, much less convince the world of it."

"You really don't believe in me?" The witch asked, even managing to look a little hurt.

"No."

"Oh, I see, I guess I'll just find some other legendary hero who opposed me to rally the people then. I know, I'll use, um, hmmmm. I think I killed all the others, this keeps happening to me. I should have killed less people, I do see that now." The witch stood up from her chair. "I know when I'm not wanted, which seems to be always. I'll just go and start a rebellion on my own. Somehow." She turned and exited out of their home. Alteem hoped it would be the last time he ever saw her, but he did not believe it. Then, just to be sure, he shouted at her retreating figure.

"Whatever you do it better not involve any baby murder!"

Chapter 6

Alteem was headed towards the school when he saw a crowd of people gathered around something. He did not have to walk much closer to see what is was, and what it was did not surprise him. The witch had stood up on a box, not being very tall, she'd then got off of the box. Walked over to a market stall, grabbed a couple more boxes, stacked them up, and then stood back up on them.

Something in Alteem told him to keep on walking by, but he had to know what she intended to do.

"Dear people of...whatever this town is."

"Santio," someone in the crowd shouted at her. Their curiosity seemed to have overcome their fear.

"I don't actually care, sorry, that's my bad though. I could see how you might think I wanted to know, but I didn't. People of Santio then, I...really rather think the time has come for you to rise up against your oppressors."

"You're our oppressor."

"No, I mean, I was but I'm not anymore. See, I was deposed, and now I want to help you. Together we can overthrow your *new* oppressors."

"You want us to help you conquer the world again?"

"That's not what I meant. I don't want to rule the world anymore, it sucked. I'm good now, no more evil."

A tomato flew out of the crowd and struck the witch in the face. It seemed her magic protected her from lethal threats, but not unlethal ones. Her eyes were wide with shock. Alteem expected anger to flare up next, but instead she looked as if she might cry.

The crowd moved away from the woman who'd thrown the tomato, a basket full of them in her arms.

"Why...why did you throw that?" the witch asked, struggling to hold back tears.

"You killed my father." The woman responded.

"I killed a lot of people's fathers, and mother's, and children. There's probably nothing I can do to make up for that, but I can help you win back your freedom."

"Go back to hell witch."

"No, because that would require me to sacrifice another baby and I've been told that's wrong, probably. Also, I don't see how that would help."

A rock flew through the crowd, there was a flash of light as it almost hit the witch and then rebounded off and flew into the crowd. The people screamed in panic, mistaking the defensive magic for hostile intent. They fled in all directions, leaving Alteem alone with the witch.

She sat on her boxes, wrapped her arms around her knees, dropped her head, and began to cry. Alteem walked over to her. She did not look up at him.

"You can't have thought that would work." Alteem said.

"Go away," the witch said in between her sobs.

"Crying isn't going to help anything."

"It won't hurt either. I've ruined my whole life, and I can never fix it. It's all my fault too. I can't even ask for sympathy after all that I've done. I am forever cursed by my own stupidity."

"I've never heard you talk like this."

"I know what I am Alteem. I see it the faces of everyone who looks at me. How could I not? Nothing I do will ever make it go away.

You're the worst of them all. Every time I look at you it's like looking into a mirror that shows me who I really am, and I'm a monster. I hate you for it. I hate you more than I've ever hated anybody, even more than my mother."

"Then why did you come to me?"

"Who else would I go to?"

Alteem did not know what else he might say. They remained there, an imperfect pair. The only sound the witch crying on her boxes. Alteem tried to summon some pity for her, or sympathy, or even compassion. He could not. Her face had been grinning as she had tortured him over and over again. She had smiled the smile of an imp as she murdered his family in front of him. She had done so to countless others. How could he pity her, but still, some part of him wished he could.

He did not know how much time had passed as he stood next to her trying to think of something to say when words managed to come from his mouth. "What's your name?"

"What?"

"Your name, no one knows it. What is it?"

"There's a reason no one knows it."

"You want a new a start. Then you have to really start over, and you can't just be 'the witch', so what's your name?"

The witch paused her crying and looked up at him. Her usual beauty tainted by her reddened eyes. "My mother named me after her favorite candy."

"You're named after candy?"

"Do you want to know it or not?"

"Sorry, go ahead."

"It's Honeydrops."

"What?"

"Honeydrops, okay, my name is Honeydrops."

"Honeydrops?"

The witch nodded.

"Plural."

"Yes."

Then, Alteem burst out into laughter. "Honeydrops, scourge of the world, swallower of nations, destroyer of empires."

"Now you know why I don't tell people."

"Okay, Honey, you can't just announce to the world you've changed. You have to prove it."

"How do I do that?"

"With all that you have done, I don't know where you could even begin."

"Will you help me?"

"I'll think about it. Right now I need to get to work."

"Teaching? Can I watch?"

"No."

Alteem went through the school day. Honeydrops always present in the back of his mind. What could be done about her? After closing the school, he looked around for her but could not find her. Walking home, he saw yet another crowd, and he immediately knew it must be her.

Pushing his way through, he saw her, sweaty in the sunlight, white paint sprinkled on her dress. She was painting a fence and the people were looking at her, some laughing as she struggled with the manual labor. Too short, she had to stand on the tips of her toes to reach the top.

"What are you doing?" Asked Alteem.

"You said I had to prove myself. I figured I had to start with something, so I asked around if I could help people with anything," Honey said.

"You can't use magic to paint the fence?"

"When my mother taught me the dark arts, amidst summoning demons, flaying people alive, sacrificing living things for power, destroying everything in my path, she left out the paint a fence spell."

"Pity, would have come in use about now."

"Are you making fun of me?" Honey sloshed some paint in his direction.

"Never."

"Meanest woman I've met, and people say I'm evil."

Alteem knew the house, and he had to admit, the witch had a point. The woman who lived there was a mean thing. She might actually be more evil than the witch, but lacked the witches power to enact that evil. It was probably not a good choice for Honey to start her path to redemption.

"There, done."

"Let's see then," Said an angry looking woman coming out from the crowd, Miss Lonsly. She was a big woman, probably bigger than Alteem, which just made her more fearsome. Many had hoped the woman might shrivel up from her cruelty in her old age, but she remained stubbornly robust. "Sloppy job, just as I figured."

"What are you talking about?" Honey protested. "I spent all day getting this perfect." The paint brush was dripping paint unnoticed on the side of her dress as she stood up.

"Bah, you're as useless as you always have been. Nothing but trouble."

"And just what is that supposed to mean?"

"You know what it means. You're trash, and you always will be. A good for nothing."

Honey's hand bent into a claw and crackled with purple light. "I have had enough of you."

The crowd that had gathered dispersed, screaming in terror. The woman fell backward, holding her hands up in a vain effort to protect herself. Alteem acted quickly, grabbing the bucket of paint he poured it over the witch's head.

The purple light vanished, and for several minutes nothing happened. Honey just stood there, shaking with rage. "Why did you do that?" She said through tight lips.

"Because you were going to kill that woman," Alteem answered.

She wiped the paint out of her eyes. "She deserves it."

"You don't get to decide who does and who does not deserve to die."

"Why not?"

"Because no one does."

"You've killed people, did they deserve to die?"

"Yes...no, I don't know. I'm not a perfect person. I didn't always do what was right, but I always tried to. There are better people in the world to use as an example of goodness."

"Who?"

Alteem considered. There was the Sisters of Charity, women who devoted their lives to helping others. They had all died in the war trying to protect people. He'd heard of a group of Monks who lived near Badell Mountain that took in everyone. They gave refuges and criminals homes and food, everyone contributed and somehow they'd made a better community then the rest of the world out of its rejects. The witch's army had swept through their home. Last Alteem had heard they were all dead. He tried to think of a few more people, but it always ended the same. "You killed them all."

"SON OF A BITCH!!! Again?" Honey fell backwards, landing on the edge of the road.

"Get up."

"No, everything sucks."

"You're just going to stay there?"

"Yes."

"For how long?"

"Forever."

"You can't stay there forever."

"I can do what I want."

"Fine."

"Fine."

The town adjusted reasonably quickly to having an all-powerful witch lying in one of their streets. It's not the sort of thing people expect to happen, but what can one do. A sign was put up reading, 'Witch Here, Careful', and people went about their business.

The paint on her dried, and made an earie white mask on her face. She just lay there, blinking occasionally. Dust gathered on her, and washed away with the rain. People wondered about her eating and... other things. Eventually everyone had to chalk it up to magic and move on. Over time, and several rainy days, she'd sunk into the earth a little.

The snows came, and all that could be seen was a small mound in the snow. It was a good thing someone had thought to put up the sign, or someone might have tripped over her in the snow. Some wondered if she'd still be there when the snow melted, and she was, lying in a puddle of mud and slush.

Her expression had changed now. Before she'd looked lost and hopeless, staring at nothing, now it looked as if she was thinking about something. As to what she was thinking, no one could say. I guess I could say, I'm writing the story after all, but I'm not telling.

The day came when Honey spoke to a passerby. "Pardon me sir, would you mind helping me to my feet? I've sunken a bit into the earth and I don't seem to be able to move."

The man jumped with a start at the witch in the road suddenly addressing him. "Can't you just, magic yourself out?" He asked.

"I could but I'd take a good deal of the road with me, and I think I've done enough damage to the world." The man eyed her, clearly not sure what he should do. "No harm will come to you from just touching me." He still did not move.

"If I wanted any harm to come to you, being stuck in the road would not stop me."

The man reached down, and after digging her arm out a little, he managed to pull her out of the earth. A witch shaped imprint remained in the ground. Honey immediately pulled out the sign and turned it around. "That's all it says, I've been wondering about that thing for months. Anyway, thank you, that's what people say right? Thank you?"

The man nodded.

"Is there...anything I can do for you, I guess?"

"Hmmm, the thing is, I always wanted, and I know it's silly, but I always wanted to be...bigger."

"I can make you taller."

"No not like that, bigger, down there, you know, bigger."

Honey stared at the man. "There are limits to even my power," then she walked away.

Chapter 7

Alteem wiped off the chalkboard, his students gone for the day. He turned around and screamed at the horrible hag who had taken up residence in one of his chairs. Reaching for the ruler he held it up to keep the creature at bay. Then he recognized Honey.

Her hair had clumps of dirt in it, and its sharp colors had become muddied. The paint on her face had flecked away in some places, but remained intact in others. Like paint peeling off a doll that had a real person underneath.

"I see you're up and about again," Alteem said, recovering from his fright.

"Yeah," she said. "I just realized something while I was laying there."

"Oh," Alteem began packing up some of his things in a satchel. "And what's that?"

"I never told you that I was sorry."

Alteem stopped packing, and looked at the witch. Her words hit him harder than he would have thought. His hands started to shake and his heart began to pound.

"I wouldn't have meant it before even if I had said it. I doubt it counts for much now, but I am sorry. I'm sorry about everything I did to you, to everyone."

Alteem had to sit, his voice suddenly hoarse. "It means more than you know."

"Well that's all, I think I'll go back to lying down now."

"You're not going to make anything better for yourself lying in the middle of the road."

"Maybe not, but at least I can't make them worse for anybody else that way. Also it wasn't the middle of the road, it was the side."

"There is more to an apology than just saying you're sorry. The next step is to try and make it right."

"How? How could I possibly make anything right after all that I have done?"

"Perhaps you can't, but trying to is a good start."

Honey opened her mouth to say something, but then closed it again.

"We can talk about it more later, let's get you cleaned up first."

The witch didn't move until Alteem guided her out of the desk and into the street. Under normal circumstances she attracted stares where ever she went, but with her current appearance people outright gawked at her.

Alteem took her home, where Alma was waiting. Alma merely frowned at seeing them. Perhaps she'd gotten used to Honey and wasn't afraid of her anymore, or perhaps it was that even the witch had trouble looking intimidating as she was.

"I'd say you need a bath," said Alma. "But one wouldn't be enough."

Honey walked over to the table and plopped down into a chair, planting her head face first down onto the table. Dirt broke free from her hair and rolled down to the floor.

"What's her problem?" Alma asked.

"Everything sucks," said Honey.

"That's hardly a reason to spread dirt everywhere."

"Sorry."

"There's a pond with a waterfall not far from here, perhaps we could get her washed up there."

"You don't have to do anything for her if you don't want to," Alteem said.

"Can't leave her like this," Alma said grabbing the witch by her arm. Honey gave out a long moan before she got to her feet and allowed herself to be led outside again. "You can clean up here," she said to Alteem. "Since you brought her inside without thinking."

"Yes Alma," Alteem said as they left.

Once the witch was outside Alma stepped back inside quickly to grab some bathing supplies and a change of clothes. By the time she got back outside the witch had planted herself face first on the ground again. "Up, up, up." Alma said getting her back to her feet.

The two women walked the entire way in silence. Honey not wanting to talk, and Alma not sure what she could say.

The pond was surrounded by a small growth of trees and had a trickle of a waterfall. Alma pealed the witch's dress off of her and tossed it aside. "In you go," Alma said.

Honey dipped one of her toes into the pond. "It's cold."

"You're not a baby, now get in."

The witch looked at Alma with resentment for a moment but finally lowered herself into the pond. Alma grabbed soap and a brush and started to scrub the filth off the witch. She went about it in silence for a while, but the witch was very dirty and it was clear they would be there for some time yet.

"What made you decide to finally get up off the road?" Alma asked.

"I kept watching the people." Honey said.

"There has to be more to it than that."

"I lived the first few decades of my life with just me, my mother, and demons for company. She told me about other people who lived outside the swamp, but I never saw them. I just learned the ways of power. I'm human, you know, like you, hard as it may be for some to believe. The first time I saw others they seemed so fragile, like insects compared to me."

"So you've always known you were human but never felt it."

"Yes, life was easy for me to take, and all I'd known about others was what my mother had told me. They meant nothing to me. Then I watched them go by, for months, even through the snow, I used my magic to see them. They all had lives they were living."

"Lift your arms up."

The witch did as she was told. "Their lives were so small, and so were their problems, but they had so much more than I've ever had. I saw lovers looking at each other, and no one has ever looked at me like that. I saw a mother looking at her child, and no one has ever looked at me like that."

The witch stopped speaking so Alma prompted her again. "And?"

"And I snuffed them out. So many of them, so many little lives, each full of happiness, heartache, love, and longing. I never really understood it before, what I had really done. How many people just like them had I killed?"

"My first husband, Mathew's father, he died in slavery to one of the beast tribes."

"I'm sorry, I wish I could undo it all. I wish I had known better."

"You can't, not even you're that powerful. Once something is done it's done. You've killed all those people. That's why you can't just lie around moping anymore, you owe it to them. You have to do something, with all you've got. You're still alive, so you have to do something."

"I don't know what to do."

"Did you ever know your own father?"

"No."

Alma started to comb the dirt out of Honey's hair. "I don't know what you should do either...sorry I don't know your name."

The witch paused, but sighed and said, "Honeydrops."

Alma stopped mid brush, but quickly resumed. "It's a very a pretty name."

"Don't lie."

Alma gave off a small chuckle. The witch turned back to her, surprised, and gave a little smile before turning away again. It was strange for honey, giving a genuine smile. She was not sure if she had simply forgotten what it felt like, or had never known. The smile came with an emotion, one Honey could not identify. She knew the word, but since she'd never felt it before, did not know the feeling went with it. It was hope.

"There you are now, all cleaned up. Come on, I brought one of my old dresses for you." Alma held up the dress and the witch eyed it. The dress was red, the skirt wide and having thick black stripes across it.

"It's not really...me." Honey said.

"Don't be ungrateful. It's the closest thing I have that I thought would fit you. I saved it from when I was a young girl because it was one of my favorites. The one you were wearing won't be suitable ever again. Unless you've got another dress stowed away somewhere."

"I left in a hurry. I do have magic, I can make more."

"I already brought it all this way."

The witch stepped out of the pond, and Alma helped her dry off. Honey stepped into the dress and Alma pulled out an old kerchief that went with the dress to tie her hair up.

"Now look at you, with your hair covered up you look almost like any other pretty girl."

"I am **not**, like any other pretty girl," the witch frowned.

Alma laughed, "No, you're not. Pity too, with your looks you could have broken even more hearts than I did in my youth."

"Isn't breaking hearts a bad thing?"

"Yes, but you miss the feeling when you get older."

"I'm much older than you."

"Are you? You don't act like it," Alma started walking back towards the house.

"What do you mean I don't act like it?" Honey stomped after her.

"Nothing child."

"Don't call me a child," The witch pouted, with Alma laughing quietly to herself.

"Remember to behave yourself, else I'll have to give you a spanking."

"You can't spank me, my magic protects me."

"From what I've heard it only protects you from harm, and I wouldn't be trying to harm you, I'd be teaching you a lesson."

"That wouldn't work," Honey said, but she did not look very confident. "You can't talk to me like this, I'm terrifying. Empires shake with fright where I walk."

"The witch was terrifying," Said Alma. "But Honeydrops has a lot to learn."

Honey gave up, crossing her arms she marched ahead of Alma. When they arrived back at the house, Honey burst through the door and sunk down into one of the kitchen chairs. "Your wife is impossible."

Alma followed behind her, smiling.

"What's happening?" Alteem asked.

"Someone's just acting a little cranky," said Alma.

"I'm not cranky," said Honey.

Alma patted her on the head, "Of course you aren't."

Someone knocked on the door and Alteem went to answer it. "Mathew," he said upon seeing the young man.

"Father, mother," Mathew said stepping in, then he saw honey. At first he didn't recognize her and her froze in his place staring at the strange beauty in his house. The witch froze too, her eyes going wide at the way Mathew was looking at her. Then her recognized her, "Oh, it's just you."

"Mathew," said Alma. "Come in, I was about to start supper."

"Yes, good timing," Alteem said.

"Don't tease the boy."

Mathew sat down at the table, avoiding the gaze of the witch who was still awkwardly stiff. "Why did you look at me like that?" The witch asked.

"I didn't look at you in any way," Mathew said.

"Don't do it again."

"Honey," said Alma. "Come help me prepare supper."

"What? Why don't they have to help?" The witch pouted.

"Because they can't cook."

"I can't cook either."

"Maybe, but I already tried teaching them. There's still hope for you. Now come here. Alteem, Mathew, you set the table."

"Yes, Alma," said Alteem.

"Yes, Mother," said Mathew.

"She's very bossy." Honey whispered to them.

Alteem and Mathew set the table while Honey and Alma prepared dinner. After the table was set, the two men stepped outside, afraid Alma might be tempted to find more work for them.

Mathew turned to Alteem and looked out at the dying light of the evening. "Her name is Honey?"

"Honeydrops," Alteem answered, shrugging.

"Plural?"

Alteem nodded.

Inside Honey was doing very well helping Alma prepare the meal. "It's a lot like performing a demonic ritual." She said, "Only it smells better, and there's no blood. There is the tomato juice."

"Oh," Alma said. "Really? Let's just focus on this, okay?"

They finished cooking supper and Alma opened the door. "It's ready," she said.

"And there's no blood in it," Honey added cheerfully.

"Great," said Alteem. "Let's eat."

They ate with casual conversation. Honey staying mostly silent. Mathew said goodbye with one last awkward look at Honey. The three remaining each picked out different books to read till night came. Honey picked out an old children's book. "I've never seen a book that had pictures which weren't depicting some kind of animal sacrifice."

Night came, "Time for bed," Alma said.

"Goodnight," The witch said without moving.

"You too."

"Oh, I don't need to sleep, I have a spell for that. I haven't slept for over a century."

"That explains why you're so cranky. A bit of rest will be good for you."

"I'm not cranky, and I'm not going to bed."

"Bed, now," Alma pointed to the door that used to be Mathew's room.

Honey looked to Alteem, who shrugged. "This isn't fair." She stomped off, throwing the door open with a wave of her hand and slamming it behind her.

"How does it feel sending a centuries old evil goddess to her bed?" Alteem asked.

"Feels pretty good," Alma said. They laughed together. "I feel bad for her."

"I've tried, but I can still see the faces of my family as she tortured them to death. At first I didn't believe it when she showed up here, but she really is trying to do better. I just can't forget. Having her here feels like holding a viper that could turn on you at any moment."

"She wouldn't hurt us."

"I don't know. All it would take is a change of her mind and she could rip this house down around us. Don't forget she's dangerous."

"I should check on her."

"Please be careful with her."

"I'll see you in bed," Alma kissed Alteem on the cheek and then she entered the viper's den.

Honey was lying on her back above the covers, staring at the ceiling.

"You're not even trying," Alma said.

"I haven't slept in a very long time, excuse me if I'm not good at it," said Honey.

"There's probably some pajamas that will work for you in one of these drawers," Alma walked over to Mathew's old dresser. She pulled out a long shirt that would work, "Here wo go, put this on."

Honey changed quickly and Alma tucked her into the bed.

"What if I still can't sleep?" Honey asked.

"I'll sing you a lullaby," said Alma.

"What's that?"

"Hush now," said Alma and began singing.

"Stars are shining, day is gone

Moon is smiling, suns moved on

Don't you fear, don't have fright

Sleep well darling, through the night

Mother's here, nightmare's gone

Moon is smiling, suns moved on

Sleep well darling, through the night

I'll be here, to hold you tight."

Chapter 8

The witch lurched out of her bedroom. "MMMMMmmmmmmmm-mmmmmmmm," She moaned, plopping herself down at the table.

"That's what happens when you don't sleep for centuries," said Alma.

The witch gave her a dirty look.

"Don't give me that attitude little miss, or I won't make you any breakfast."

And that was how life with the witch began. It is always remarkable how quickly people can adjust to things. The town adjusted to an unstoppable witch lying in one of their roads, and Alma and Alteem adjusted to her living in their home.

The witch seemed to enjoy it, learning the sort of things other people did to live their lives. To most people magic was wonderful, but to someone who'd used magic their whole life, the ordinary was magical. She learned to sew, garden, cook, and clean. In time Alteem softened a bit to her and taught her things he knew. He gave her the sort of lessons he'd been given as child. She learned about history and science. The philosophy of the great thinkers, and he did his best to teach her about morality.

One day, as Honey was sitting reading, a knocking came at the door. Alma and Alteem weren't home at the time, so Honey thought it best to ignore it. She had been accepted into this home, but the villagers were, understandably, not fond of her.

The knocking came again, more insistent, followed by a plea. "Please," said a young woman's voice. "If you're there, witch, I need your help."

The witch got to her feet and moved to the door. She opened it just enough for one eye to peek out. A woman stood before her, dark hair and dark eyes. Fear flashed across the woman's face upon seeing Honey, but she fought it down.

"Whatever the price," said the woman. "I will pay it, but I need your help."

"I won't paint anymore fences," said Honey.

"What? No, my son is dying, the doctor cannot save him. But you have magic don't you, there must be a way for you to help."

"No," said Honey, the woman's face turning to despair at hearing the word. "I can't, I was never taught how to heal."

"Please," said the woman. "If anyone can help it's you. I will do anything."

"I told you, I don't know how, I'm sorry," Honey started to close the door.

The woman pushed it open and grabbed her by the hand, she was crying. "Please, just see him, there must be something you can do, just see him."

Honey stared at the woman holding her hand. People had pleaded with her many times, but always at a distance. She'd killed anyone who got too close to her. The witch did not recall the last time someone had held her hand like this, or if anyone ever had. How easy it would have been, not that long ago, to say no. She would have thought nothing of this woman and her child. "I will go with you, but I tell you now, there is nothing I can do."

"Thank you," The woman said. She dragged honey by the hand as if she was afraid the witch might vanish the moment she let go.

They arrived at the woman's house, only one room with hard clay for walls. Inside an older gentleman stood beside a bed. In the bed was a boy, whose skin was pallid and dripping with sweat. The whole room smelled of sick and vomit.

"You brought her then," said the Doctor. "A mistake trusting a witch."

"Can you help him?" The woman asked.

The witch knelt down beside boy and felt his head. He was hot with fever. "I told you, there's nothing I can do, save give him a painless end."

The woman broke into tears, falling down at the foot of her son's bed.

"You're magic is not endless then?" The doctor asked.

"No," said Honey. "There is magic I was never taught."

"Is it not possible for you to learn some healing magic?"

"I...the only source of spells I know is my family's grimoire. I have made spells of my own, but it takes time and practice. I doubt there would be healing magic inside the grimoire. For generations my family has only tried to conquer the world."

"Why?"

"It seems like a good idea before you try it."

The woman managed to choke out some words, "Can you not look, just to be certain there is nothing you can do?"

"I'd need a knife."

Nodding, the woman went to her kitchen and grabbed a knife. She handed it to the witch. Honey knelt and held out her free hand to the woman. "You're hand." The woman placed her hand in hers and Honey used the knife to draw a thin cut across her palm. Using the woman's bleeding hand she drew a circle and several ruins on the floor. "That's enough," said Honey, and the doctor went about bandaging the hand.

Honey placed her own hand in the center of the circle and mumbled a spell. The blood turned to black flame and a portal of fire appeared on the floor. Reaching through the portal, Honey pulled an imp through and it closed behind the creature.

The imp was less than two feet tall, a hunched and twisted creature that had one talon and one goat leg. Three eyes looked around the room, two on the left side and one on the right, but the right eye was so sunken into the skull and it could barely be seen. Its ears were long and pointed, but one dripped down to its shoulder. Its skin was a mix of flesh and translucent scales. Through the scales its blood could be seen pumping with every heartbeat.

"Ah, ah, mistress, how have you been?" The imp said.

"Oh, I've been just terrible Fredrick, but I don't have time to tell you about it. I need you to fetch my grimoire."

"Yes mistress," the imp snapped its fingers and vanished in a puff of flame.

The witch sat back while they waited, the only sound that of the mother's occasional sobs. Honey never knew how long it might take to fetch the grimoire, so there was no choice but to wait. The Doctor cleared his throat and the witch started to twiddle her fingers.

"So," said the Doctor. "Did you, usually have demons run your errands when you were ruler of the world?"

"No, on account of the blood requirement. It was usually just easier to get a minion to do something. Do you ever have demons run errands for you?"

"No, not a lot of demon summoning in medicine."

"Right, I suppose not. So...um...hmmm."

"What?"

"Nothing, nothing."

"Hmmm, magic then."

"What about it?"

"Is it difficult?"

"Like any skill, best if you have natural talent for it but anyone could do a little."

"Ah."

"Yes." The witch idly looked around.

"...I've heard you're immortal then."

"Yes, well, ageless actually. I can be killed but only by strong magic."

"Do you get sick?"

"The sniffles sometimes, but only around spring."

"Could just be allergies."

"Really? You think?"

"Maybe."

"Oh."

Honey started to tap her foot on the floor.

"Could you not?" Asked the doctor.

"Sorry."

"Are you the only witch?"

"No, I killed off most of them so they couldn't threaten me, but I left one of each coven so they could recover in time."

"Do you belong to a coven?"

"There's always only been mother and daughter in my coven. Once there was more but they were all killed and it became a tradition for each generation to raise a child to be stronger than the last. If the child wasn't then they would be killed and another child would be had."

"I see."

"What made you want to be a doctor?"

"You did."

"Oh really, how?"

"I saw so much death and suffering under your reign of terror it made me want to do something to help people."

"Mmm."

"What made you want to conquer the world?"

"Family tradition."

"And how did that get started."

"Something about revenge, I never really listened to that part."

"For all the other witches in your coven who were killed?"

"Oh, maybe, yeah, could be."

There was a flourish of flame and the imp appeared, a leather book in his hands.

"You're back," said Honey. "That took you forever."

"It was only a couple of minutes," said Frederick.

"Was it really, it felt much longer than that."

"A healing spell," the mother said.

"Of course, yes, you're dismissed Frederick."

Another flourish of flame and the imp was gone, the book falling to the floor. Honey waved her hand and it flew open, its pages unfolding into a grid. The pages of the grid each flipped around, revealing new pages as they leapt over each other. Shapes and words formed in the grid only to change as the pages changed.

The grimoire was a record of the magic practiced by all the witches in her family who had ever lived. There were spells to kill, spells to torture, control, or manipulate. Spells new and ancient, all hidden in a maze that only those who knew how could even start to traverse. Honey knelt before it, watching the pages shift across each other, searching for something new, something she'd never seen before. She went back further in time, perhaps there was a time before her family had turned to death.

Memories of magic flitted before her eyes and time slipped away, as it often did when perusing the grimoire. It was like stepping out of reality. Most people would just see it as gibberish, but if you knew what to look for it was a sea of knowledge. Diagrams of dissections used in rituals, passages where the rules of the universe were charted long ago.

She looked through the maze, searching in all directions for things she'd never seen before. Some clue, some trail, to magics not conjured since times before the memories of humanity. There was something here, something about a tree she did not know. Willow and oak branches, mashed with red petals. It wasn't a healing spell, but it was a spell Honey had never seen before. Was this the way?

It was a strange place to her, this part of the grimoire. Not full of death, blood, and darkness. It felt green and full of light. A different sort of magic not accessed for generations, a sort of magic she had never looked for. It felt as if it was glad to see her.

"I need," said Honey. "Yellowgrass or honeywheat, and a silver chain."

"There's yellowgrass grows not far from here," said the mother. "I can go fetch it, but I have no silver."

"I can get a silver chain," said the doctor hurrying towards the door.

The two left, leaving the witch alone. "I'll just wait here then." She shouted after them. Since she'd gone to the trouble of fetching her grimoire, she decided to spend the time seeing what else she might discover. There were so many new magics in this part of the tome.

The doctor returned a few minutes later, placing a thin silver chain next to Honey. She did not move from examining the ever changing grid of the grimoire. It took much longer for the mother to return. When she at last arrived, she held out a fistful of yellowgrass to Honey, who took it from her. The tome closed back up into its book form.

Honey went about weaving the yellowgrass into the chain. Despite the small size of the chain, the witches hands were deft and the work went quickly. Soon the grass was interwoven through the entire chain, and Honey went over to the boy, placing it around his neck.

She held her hand over the boy and closed her eyes. A purple glow began to emanate from her hands, growing brighter and larger with each second. Soon the boy and witch were enveloped in the glow.

The light burst outward, giving a small pulse that caused the house to shutter. The doctor and mother were knocked off balance. When they recovered they saw the witch lying passed out on the floor, and the boy began to stir.

"Nicolas," said the mother. She threw her arms around the boy as he sat up in his bed. He had a sort of tattoo around his neck now, gold and silver intertwined together.

The doctor went to the witch, he checked her pulse to make sure she was alright. Satisfied she was fine for the moment, he checked on the boy. His hand went to the boy's forehead. "Fever's gone. Keep an eye on him for the next few days, but it seems the magic has worked. Bring him by tomorrow, I'll give him a full checking over just to be sure."

The doctor went back to the witch, carefully turning her onto her back. She had a gash on her forehead leaking blood. She'd likely hit the edge of something on her way to the floor. The doctor went his bag to grab some stitching equipment. By the time he was back to the witch she was waking up.

Her hand went to her head as her eyes opened. "There's something warm leaking down." She said as she examined her fingertips. "Blood?" Confusion spread across the witches face. "MY BLOOD!" She bolted upright and glanced around. Seeing them, she scampered to the corner, her hands went up and started to crackle with purple energy. Then she stopped sinking back down to the floor seeming to remember what happened.

"It's alright," said the doctor. He approached her carefully with the kit. "I can stitch that right up."

She nodded, and he knelt beside her. She was shaking, the doctor thought to ask why her magic hadn't protected her, but perhaps it only protected from others harming her. It would not stop her from hitting her own head on something. He brought the needle to her forehead, and she eyed it nervously. He paused, wondering if her magic might destroy the needle. "Will your magic, stop it?"

"Only if you mean to harm me," the witch said, her voice shaking as much as her body.

"This will sting a bit," he said.

Honey winced every time the needle made its way through her skin, a sharp pain that quickly eased but returned just as quickly.

"If you had warned me about you passing out as side effect of the spell, we might have been able to catch you."

"That wasn't because of the spell, that was because I made a small mistake. Magic is tricky, usually I'd go over a spell mentally for a week before attempting it. One time when I messed up a spell I vaporized everything within a mile around me. Good thing that didn't happen this time."

"Right, good thing." said the doctor. "All finished. It should heal in a couple of days. Though there will likely be a small scar."

"What? I can't have a scar, my face is perfect. It's the only good thing about me."

The doctor's eyes glanced to where the mother was still hugging her son. "Not anymore," he said.

Chapter 9

Mathew was on his way to his mother's house when he saw the witch in a field. Part of him told himself to keep walking, but he couldn't help being curious. She was on her knees with her hands outstretched, glowing purple. He traveled over to her.

"What are you doing out here, Honey?" Mathew asked her.

"Don't bother me, I'm concentrating," The witch said, dismissing him.

"Concentrating on what?"

"Shush!" She said to him, then there was the sound of wood groaning against itself. A sapling emerged from the ground, stretching upwards until it was no longer a sapling. Mathew scrambled back as the tree tore up the ground around them, it's roots rapidly spreading. The witch got to her feet as the tree grew and she stepped backward slowly as it invaded her space. Then it stopped. "Hah!" The witch exclaimed, turning on her feet. "No magic is beyond me."

The tree was probably large enough to be a hundred years old.

"You just grew a tree." Mathew said.

"I know, I was here when it happened. I wonder if I can grow an entire forest." Said Honey.

"You can't just grow an entire forest where ever you please."

"Not yet no, but give me a couple days and, BAM, forests everywhere." The witch started to walk towards home.

"That's not what I mean." Mathew said following her. "There could be serious ecological consequences if you just start making forests everywhere."

"Like what?"

"For one, areas that are too dry cause frequent forest fires. Secondly I don't think I've even seen that kind of tree before. It could replace native tree populations which might create serious problems for the local wildlife."

"Like what?"

"I don't know, that's the problem."

"Alright, fine, I'll be careful."

"That's, no, no forests at all. When did you start making trees?"

"Today. I've been practicing for a while."

Mathew looked at Honey, "Do you have scar?"

"No," The witch said, and started to walk faster.

"How did you get a scar, aren't you supposed to be impervious to harm."

"I hit my head, the magic only protects me from other people harming me. Not from self-harm."

"Pretty free with your secrets."

"It's not like someone can make me harm myself."

"What if someone slipped you a drug that made you sleepy and led you to the edge of a cliff?"

"The drug wouldn't work."

"Really, so drugs don't work on you."

"Not unless I take them on purpose."

"Fascinating, so you could get drunk?"

"I have been drunk."

"It's difficult to imagine."

"I don't make good decisions when I'm drunk."

"You don't make good decisions when you're sober."

"Then you can imagine how bad the decisions I make when I'm drunk are."

"Like what?"

"I don't want to talk about it," Honey arrived at the house. Opening the door, she closed it behind her, forcing Mathew to open it for himself. "I grew a whole tree today," Honey said to Alma as Mathew entered the house.

"Good for you," said Alma.

"I think I'll grow a whole forest next."

"Mother," said Mathew. "If she's not careful she could cause serious ecological harm."

"Well, I'm sure she'll be careful," said Alma.

"She wasn't today."

"Honey, do you promise to be careful when growing forests?"

"I promise," Honey said while rolling her eyes.

"She didn't mean that," said Mathew.

"I'm sure she meant it," said Alma.

Mathew looked over at the witch who stuck her tongue out at him. "You're not very mature for an all-powerful being, you know that."

"Blah, blah, blah de blah," said Honey.

"Be nice, you two," said Alma.

"Sorry Alma," said Honey.

"Sorry Mother," said Mathew.

"Honey, would you be a dear and peel those potatoes for me," said Alma.

The witch waved her hand over the potatoes. Their outer skin went flying off in all directions. A purple glow caught the skins and placed them in the trash bin.

"You have a spell for peeling potatoes?" Mathew asked.

"I have a spell for taking the skin off of things," said Honey.

"Oh."

"Want to see me slice some cucumbers?"

Mathew did not answer her, instead, he engaged his mother in small talk. He did his best to ignore the witch for the rest of evening. He would not see her again until a few days later when he stepped outside his door to find her waiting for him.

"Come on," she said. "I've got something to show you."

"I can't go now," said Mathew. "I've got to go to work."

"Didn't you go to work yesterday?"

"I work five days a week."

"Why on earth would you do that?"

"Because that's what adults do."

"Well then adults are stupid."

"I don't have the time to explain this to you," Mathew headed towards his office, praying to any gods that might be the witch wouldn't follow him. Clearly there weren't any gods.

"What do you do all day?" The witch asked.

"I've been handling a lot of divorces lately. Since the end of the world has been postponed people are less afraid of dying alone and divorce rates have gone up."

"That's depressing."

"In one respect yes, but if you think about, high divorce rates indicate that people feel they have more options and mobility in society. So really they're an indication of a more liberal, free, and economically healthy society."

"I tried to make a spell to make people who love each other hate each other."

"Did it work?"

"Yes, but it was much too difficult a spell. It's a lot easier to do it without magic."

Mathew had to laugh at that. The witch gave him a quizzical look. She did not seem to understand why he'd laughed. "Ever do any spells to make people fall in love?"

"Falling in love is easy, the tricky part is staying in love. Sometimes no amount of magic is enough."

"Did you ever make anyone love you?"

"No, what would be the point of being loved if it wasn't real."

"Is that why you play house with Father and Mother, you like to pretend someone could love you?"

Honey glared at him, it was the sort of glare that said she would kill him if she wasn't currently on a no murder policy. Mathew decided not to pursue the question further. It did shut her up while she followed him to the office.

Today was mostly paper work, with Honey watching him the entire time. "Don't you have something you'd rather be doing?" He asked her.

"I've had a lot of free time since giving up control of the world."

"That would clear up a person's schedule."

"Do you do this all day?"

"No, sometimes I have meetings with clients, or judges, or other lawyers."

"Can we do that instead, because watching you do this is boring."

"No, I don't have any meetings today."

The witch let out a whine and then laid down on the floor. Every fifteen minutes or so she would let out a long, "Booooooooorrrrreed."

Mathew did his best to ignore her. He got up from his desk for lunch and the witch jumped to her feet, "Are we done?"

"No, it's just lunch. There's another four hours of work after that"

"WHAT!? You're only halfway done." She crawled onto his desk and grabbed him by the collar. "Why do you live like this? It's inhuman."

"You would know a lot about inhumanity given the countless innocents you slaughtered."

"Exactly, and I'm telling you this is like a form of torture. I would have forced people to do this as punishment if I'd have thought of it."

"You must have had clerks to run administrative stuff for you when you ruled the world."

"I did, I'm just now realizing I never truly appreciated them. I wonder if it would be inopportune to send them a gift basket, or maybe a succubus."

"Don't succubuses...is it succubuses or succubi?"

"Succubi."

"Don't succubi steal people's souls?"

"There's no way they can still have souls after working like this for so long. It would just be good clean fun for them. Maybe not clean."

"Okay, it just so happens I enjoy my work."

"Really? Are you mentally ill? Here, I've been learning about healing, maybe I can help," Honey reached her hands up on either side of Mathew's head but he pushed them away.

"I am not mentally ill."

The witch paused, her eyes looking with doubt upon him. "It would only take a second."

"I'm going to lunch."

"Can't we go do my thing first?"

"I don't even know what your thing is."

"Then come and find out."

Mathew gave a drawn-out sigh. "If for no other reason than to get rid of you."

The witch yipped and grabbed his hand, leading the way. They left the town, and walked for several minutes into pathless wilderness.

"How far is it exactly?"

"A few of hours outside of town."

"You didn't tell me that."

"Does it matter?"

"It's going to take up the rest of my work day."

"You're welcome."

Mathew thought it better not to argue. He eventually wrenched his hand free but continued to follow her. The journey was not quite as long as the witch had claimed, but still took nearly two hours. They stood at the edge of a valley, lush and green from the river running through it.

"There used to be a forest here," Honey said. "It was clear cut."

"So?"

"You said if I grew a forest in the wrong place it would be ecologically disastrous. So, if I grow one where there used to be a forest, and only grow indigenous trees it will be fine."

Mathew wanted to yell at her for dragging him out here for this, but he didn't think it would do him any good. "Fine," he said. "Grow your forest."

The witch yipped again. Her hands began to glow purple and she shoved them into the earth. She closed her eyes as she knelt on all fours. Nothing happened for several minutes, then the river began to glow. Nothing for as many minutes again, and the earth began to rumble.

Trees sprouted, hundreds of them all across the valley. Their wood moaned as they stretched upwards. The sound of it became so intense Mathew covered his ears. A dendrological symphony that croaked towards the sky. Then it fell silent.

The witch pulled her hands from the ground. She was drenched in sweat, and some of the dirt clung to her hands. Wiping her forehead, she left a smear of mud across it. She got to her feat, and began to laugh. No, not laugh, it was a cackle, an evil cackle that echoed across the now forested valley. She stretched her hands to the sky and purple lighting arched upwards, overwhelming the sun for an instant with its dark glow.

"Soon," Honey said, her voice twisted and raw. "Soon I will cover the entire earth in a wave of unstoppable vegetation."

"Is that your new evil plan then?"

Honey jumped, startled by his voice. She lowered her hands and smoothed her dress. "Shut up," she pouted. "It was just a reflex."

"Most people's reflexes aren't to destroy the world after every major accomplishment."

"I'm doing my best, this 'being good' stuff doesn't come easily to me."

Mathew looked out across the valley. "It's a very nice forest," He said.

Chapter 10

The witch was sitting on the floor, she had a plant before her. She held her hand up and it would grow upwards, then she turned her hand and made a fist. The plant blackened and withered. She repeated the process over and over again. "I now have power over life and death," she whispered to herself.

"That's nice dear," Alma said, who was sitting knitting a sweater for the witch since the cold season was approaching.

A knock came at the door. "Could you be a sweetheart and answer it?" Alma asked.

Honey got up from her plant and answered the door.

A portly man stood before her. His head was bald and his remaining hair a bowl of black.

"Are you here for Alteem or Alma?" The witch asked.

"Well...the thing is, I'm here for you. See, I have this growth, and I've heard you could heal people." The man lifted up his shirt to reveal a black mass on the side of his body.

Honey closed the door.

"That was rude," said Alma. "You should help that man."

"It was gross," said Honey.

"That's no excuse."

"But, it was really gross."

"Open the door, Honey."

"I feel like, you're maybe not listening. I really need you to hear me right now. It was very, like, really super gross."

Alma put her hands on her hips.

"But..."

Alma raised her eyebrow.

"But-" ·

Alma raised her eyebrow even further.

"Fine, I'll do it," Honey stomped her feat all the way to the door. She opened it and the saw the man was already walking away. "Oh, look at that, he's leaving. Well I tried."

Alma cleared her throat.

"Sir, sir, please come back," Honey called out to the man.

The man hurried back over to her.

"I guess I'll help you," she told him.

"Oh thank you, thank you so much."

"Here's how this is going to happen. I'm going to hold out my hand close my eyes. You're going to back up the growth into my hand and I'll make it disappear." The witch covered her eyes with one of her hands. "And!" She yelled pulling her hand back for a moment. "If it ends up touching any other part of your body, that part will end up disappearing. Do I make myself clear?"

"Yes ma'am, very clear."

"It'll disappear forever, just gone. I ain't bringing it back."

"Right, right."

"Okay, let's do this." She closed her eyes and turned away, her face scrunching up in trepidation. She held her hand out and felt something touch it. "Ew, ew, ew." She said as she worked her wondrous power.

The spell was over and the man stepped away. "Thank you so much," he said. "You may have save-"

"No, don't talk. Just go and let me forget this ever happened."

"I'll never forget miss, whatever they may say about you. You're a hero to me."

"Really?"

"Yes, thank you again, and goodbye."

The witch felt an unfamiliar swelling in her chest. "That was, actually very touching. Ew, touching, why'd I use that word? I think I need a bath." Closing the door, she twirled her hand and a golden bath appeared in the middle of the house.

"Honey!" Alma yelled, "What did I tell you about summoning baths in the middle of the house?"

Honey paused looking sheepishly at her feet. "I don't remember."

"Honey." Alma said with warning on her voice.

"You might have said, not to."

"You've shown you're perfectly capable of creating temporary pocket dimensions to take baths in."

"But that's so much work," Honey whined.

"Well it's that or take a bath in a normal bathtub."

"I could just make you a bigger a house. Granted, if my history is any indication the architecture might not make any sense, but it would be quite bigger."

"I told you before, Honey, I prefer my architecture logical."

"Pfff, spatial reality is so over rated."

"Well little lady, not all of us grew up traveling through chaos realms. Call me old fashioned, but I prefer to know what's going to be on other side of a door when I walk through it. Or at the very least that I'll still on the same plane of existence."

"Have it your way, if you need me I'll be outside creating a temporary separate reality."

An hour or so later another knock came at the door. Alma answered to see an old lady with a cane standing before her. "Hello, Gladis," Alma said.

"I hope this was the right door to knock on," Gladis said. "I didn't expect there to be two doors so I decided to knock on the one that had a building attached to it. Also it wasn't swirling with darkness."

Alma leaned out of the house to see better. Sure enough, there was a door standing up in her yard unsupported. It was black with three red windows in a triangular pattern. A haze of darkness drifted around it. "Honey is just in there taking a bath."

"Who's Honey?"

"The witch."

"Oh," Gladis nodded before looking up at her. "Her name is Honey?"

Alma just shrugged. "Honeydrops, but we call her Honey for short."

"Well she's the one I'm here to see. I've heard she's been healing people, and well, my knees have been troubling me quite a bit lately."

"Alright Gladis, we'll see if she can help you." Alma took Gladis over to Honey's door and knocked on it. A moment later honey opened the door, completely naked and dripping wet.

"What!?" Honey said, her face impatient with anger.

"You're naked," said Alma.

"Yeah," Honey said. "I'm in the middle of a bath, which you knew."

"You can't go about answering doors naked, especially when we have company."

"Oh, I don't mind," said Gladis, eyeing the witch up and down.

"Why not?" Protested the witch.

"It's indecent." Said Alma.

"Why?"

"It just is?"

"I trusted you guys on the whole baby killing thing, but you're not making a strong argument for this one."

"You wouldn't go naked any other time of the day."

"No, I wouldn't, but I'm taking a bath right now. Which I said already. Plus I like pretty dresses, I left a lot of them behind when I left

78

my palace. I had this one which felt like silk, but it wasn't. See I used my magic to make it out of the skins of-" Honey paused. "Nevermind what it was made of. What's that, put some clothes on you say, okay." Honey slammed the door with Gladis leaning over to get a view for as long as possible.

"So Gladis, I had no idea that were into, um-"

"The ladies, no need to be shy about it woman. I'm not ashamed. Let's just say my knees are sore for a reason."

"I didn't need you to tell me that Gladis."

Gladis cackled and Alma couldn't help but wonder if she was part witch too.

"I've seen some lookers in my time, but that Honey, 'ey?"

"I don't want to talk about this."

"I could've died right then and there and been a happy woman."

"Gladis, please."

"Don't tell me you've never made a move on her. I know you're not like that, but someone that beautiful has to tempt even you."

"You're doing this to me on purpose aren't you?" Alma frowned at the old woman.

"An old lady has to keep herself entertained somehow?"

"Isn't that how you said your knees got sore?"

Gladis cackled again.

The door opened again with the witch now clothed and dry.

"That was fast," said Gladis.

"Like magic," said Honey. She stepped outside of the door and it disappeared behind her. "What was so important it had to interrupt my bath?"

"Gladis was hoping you could help with the pain in her knees," said Alma.

The witch glared at them both for several seconds. "I feel this could have waited until after my bath," she said at last.

"You didn't have to close your little dimension thingy."

"First off, it's called a pocket dimension, and I know you know that. Moreover yes, yes I did have to close it. Sometimes it's like you know nothing about manipulating reality."

"I don't."

"Well maybe if you made a little effort to learn about these things we wouldn't find ourselves in these situations."

"I promise in the future I won't make you leave any alternative dimensions unless it's an emergency. Does that make you feel better?"

"Yes it does."

"Good, now can we help Gladis?"

Honey bent down and placed a hand on Gladis's knee. She straightened again, "It's not a disease or illness, but just the result of the natural aging process. My grimoire warned about interfering with the natural aging of things lest there be horrific consequences."

Gladis dropped her head in disappointment.

"Eh," said Honey. "What's the worst that could happen?" She started to bend down again but Alma put a hand on her shoulder to stop her.

"What is the worst that can happen?" Alma asked.

"The book was somewhat vague on that, but if I had to take a guess I'd say...zombieism."

"What is that?"

"It's not so bad, just the dead rising from their graves to consume the living."

"That sounds like a fate worse than death?" said Gladis.

"Sooooooooooooo...yes, no?" The witch shrugged her shoulders.

"No," said Alma.

"Then I'll just have to whip up a potion to help with the pain. I'll need to get a cauldron and a fire going."

The witch started to walk around the house when Alma called after her. "Make sure it doesn't have any terrible consequences that go along with it."

"Good thing you reminded me about that because I would *not* have remembered."

More people would arrive at the door, some because they needed healing, others because they'd heard there was a chance to see the witch naked. None were so lucky again, more from Alma's carefulness than Honey's.

Word spread, and people from further and further away began to arrive at the door. With people, came rumors from afar.

Chapter 11

“War,” said Mathew. “It’s coming, and coming soon.”

“I was really good at war,” said Honey.

“Not everything is about you,” said Alteem.

“I know, but I wish it was.”

“Where?” Alteem asked.

“Everywhere, from what people are saying,” said Mathew.

“Not here,” said Alteem. “And let’s hope it stays that way.” He’d known it was coming. Without the witch to hold her empire together it was inevitable things would fracture and split. People would fight, for whatever stupid reasons they always fought. After so much loss and pain, the last thing the world needed was more wars. Then, it never needed wars, but that never stopped anyone.

“Why not let it come?” Said Mathew. “This is a chance for a country of our own. Now is the time.”

“Do you remember war Mathew? You were very young the last time there was one. I know enough dead people. Everyone I ever loved or cared about was torn away from me. They’re gone forever, and for what?”

“That does sound terrible when you put it that way,” said the witch. Alteem gave her a sour look. “I already apologized, what more do you want for me.”

“I want all my loved ones back from the dead.”

"Not a good idea, bringing people back from the dead, for a whole number a reasons. Not the least of which is the smell."

"But your war was a just one, Alteem. You fought to protect people from the greatest evil the world had ever known," said Mathew.

"That's a good a point," said the witch.

Mathew and Alteem glared at her.

"I've always admitted that I was evil. I was great at it too, shame it didn't work out for me. Don't look at me like that, it just feels nice to know you were the best in the world at something. You two clearly can't relate."

"As I was saying," said Mathew, casting one more glance at Honey. "There are things worth fighting for, worth dying for."

"The world would be better off if people found things to live for instead. Take it from a man who's been to hell and back." Said Alteem.

"You've never to been to hell," said the witch. "I've been to hell, dreadful place."

"I was speaking figuratively."

"Oh..."

"Stop interrupting."

Honey crossed her arms and pouted.

"War doesn't need two consenting parties to happen," said Mathew. "People are already fighting, it's happening. If we don't fight now, all chance we have of freedom could be swept away from us."

Alteem looked at the witch, she seemed to be winning an imaginary argument with him in her head. "Perhaps we can have that and avoid fighting. No one would dare oppose the witch. If we used her to stop these wars before they got out of hand, we could ensure a peaceful transition to whatever new nations may emerge in the world. Will you help us Honey?"

Honey did not answer, she just sat where she was, tapping her fingers against her knee.

"It's not interrupting if someone is directly addressing you?"

"You only ever like to talk to me when you want something from me," said Honey.

"It's difficult to make casual conversation with the person who destroyed my entire life and tortured me until I lost track of the days."

"I know all that, but it would be nice if you at least made an effort. I do have feelings as you so often seem to forget."

"Honey, please, sit at the table."

The witch got to her feet and slid into one of the chairs. She crossed her legs and placed her hands upon her knees.

"Listen carefully," said Alteem. "I hate you, and always will."

"But-"

"Always. There may be those out there who could endure all that you have done to me and find a way to forgive you. I am not one of them. I do not know whether it is wisdom or compassion I lack. Every time I see you I want to strangle you. You are a constant reminder of the absolute anguish you caused in my life. The only reason I have tolerated your presence is because I believe you are sincere in your desire to do better."

Alteem reached out and grabbed one of the witch's hands. "This is a real chance to do something. Not to make the world right again. Not to set things back to what they were, but put everything on the right course. We have the opportunity to make a better world, a better path for humanity to follow. No more princes, kings, and witches, just people doing their best together as equals."

"I don't know," said the witch. "Sounds like an awful lot of work."

"What's this really about?"

"Being here is the closest I've ever been to being happy. I don't want to leave."

"It's not about what you want. You said you want to be good. It's not enough to just abandon evil. When it comes to the prevention of suffering, inaction is sometimes tantamount to guilt. This is one of those times. You can save countless lives, and put this world back in order."

"Do I have to?"

"Yes."

"Ugh, fine I'll do it." The witch pulled her hand away.

"First we need a plan."

"Ooo, ooo," the witch raised her hand excitedly. "I have a plan."

"We need a plan that *doesn't* involve baby sacrifice."

"Never mind then," Honey put her hand back down.

"Sergei Haffleford," said Mathew.

"What?"

"He wrote the manifesto against the witch. The man's a visionary, if anyone could come up with a better model of government than the old monarchies it would be him."

"You're saying if we find him he can help us."

"Exactly."

"Road trip," Honey stood up excitedly. "I love road trips."

"When were you ever on a road trip?" asked Mathew.

"When I conquered the world, obviously."

"You marched across it with and army, was that really a road trip?"

"I was on the road, it was a trip. Just because I had an army and killed everyone doesn't disqualify it. We didn't actually use many roads though, as I said earlier I had no idea there were so many. Now I think of it, I could probably have conquered the world a lot faster if we had used roads. Where are we going?" She leaned forward in anticipation.

"Melscen." Mathew said.

"That place is a shithole." The witch slouched back into her chair.

"After you destroyed it."

"How it became a shithole is not important right now, a shithole is a shithole."

"People have been rebuilding it to be the hub of intellectual pursuit."

"Oooo, this is Melscen, we're so smart, we won't bow down to a despotic tyrant, pfff, I showed them," The witch paused. "Now that I think about it, I might not be that welcome in Melscen. Maybe we can go somewhere friendlier to me like...um...um...oh, right. Do I *really* have to do this?"

"Are you certain Segei would help us?" Alteem asked.

"He's one of the most brilliant men alive. Of course he will," said Mathew. "We should leave as soon as we're able."

"I guess we're just ignoring my feelings then. It's fine, I'm used to it." said Honey.

"Nothing is certain yet, we still need to discuss it with Alma," said Alteem.

"Discuss what with me?" Alma said entering the room.

"We're going on a road trip," said Honey.

"Where to?"

"We haven't decided for sure yet." Said Honey.

"Melscen," said Mathew.

"Why Melscen?" Asked Alma.

"Sergei Haffleford, if anyone will know how to avert disaster in the coming conflicts, it will be him."

"You're all just going to leave me here alone?"

"No," said Honey. "You have to come with us. She's coming with us right?"

"I've never been more than a few miles away from this village. I couldn't possibly go all the way to Melscen." Said Alma

"That's perfect, we don't have to go straight to Melscen. There's all kinds of great stuff we can stop by to see along the way. There's the crossing spears of Almara, the world's largest Wagon Wheel at Shata-cawa, the silver archway of Sintagon, wait, I might have destroyed that one."

"I thought the world's largest Wagaon Wheel was at Mordenst." Said Alteem.

"Not anymore," said Honey.

"What happened to Mordenst?"

"I did."

"Of course."

"What do you say Alma?" Asked the Witch.

"I just don't know," said Alma. "This is my home, it's always been my home."

"She doesn't have to come," said Mathew.

"Yes she does," said Honey.

"Why?"

"Because she's the only one who's ever nice to me."

"Alright," said Alma, patting the witch on her shoulder. "If you can be brave enough to change, so can I."

"FAMILY ROAD TRIP!" The witch shrieked with excitement. "I'll go pack." The witch snapped her fingers and a small black bag appeared in a whirl of purple smoke. "Done, let's go." She got halfway up then sat back down. "I have to wait for the rest of you I suppose."

"We'll have to wait a week or so to put our affairs in order." Said Alteem.

"A week, but I already packed."

"That's your own fault for being too eager."

"I can't believe I have to unpack again. You people think magic is so easy, but can any of you do it? No." The witch waved her hand and her purse disappeared into purple mist.

"*Can* anyone do magic?" Mathew asked.

"That's not the point," the witch said, sitting back down and crossing her arms.

"What is the point?"

"That magic is hard. You all take it for granted that I can do anything, but that doesn't mean it's easy to do it. I literally just summoned and dismissed an entire new dimension by my side in a convenient and fashionable handbag. None of you even care."

"You're right, I don't care. The handbag wasn't that fashionable either." Mathew said.

"I have my own style. I'm a leader not a follower. Not just of the world, which I used to be, but in fashion as well. Trend setter, that's what I am."

"In order to be a trend setter, other people have to follow your trends. I've never seen anyone else dress like you."

"I'll have you know, my style is very popular in Hell, and also in a set of planar vortexes called the Agony Dimensions. You've probably never heard of it."

"You probably just made it up."

"I'd show you," said the witch crossing her arms. "But you'd go insane forever if I took you there for even one second. If you don't mind becoming a drooling vegetable, then I'd gladly take you for a visit."

"How convenient I can't go anywhere your style is actually popular."

"No then? Figures you'd chicken out."

"Fine, I'm calling your bluff. Take me there." Mathew leaned forward on the table.

"I wasn't serious about taking you." The witch rolled her eyes.

"I knew it, not a real place."

"Alma, Alteem, talk some sense into him," Honey looked around. "Huh, they both left, wonder when that was."

"Probably around the time you started making up dimensions."

"I didn't make it up."

"Yup, sure, I believe you."

"Fine, I'll take you, I just need you to sign a waiver freeing me from all responsibility." A page and quill appeared on the table.

Mathew picked up the paper and read it.

> This Document states that Honey is not liable for any loss
> of sanity, limbs, soul, and/or pants of the signer.

Mathew signed along the line at the bottom. "There you are," he said, handing the paper to the witch.

"I'm warning you, you'll regret this."

"I don't think I will."

The witch drew an oval in the air with her finger, a crackling purple energy appearing as she did so. When the circle was complete, a tunnel of whirling purple lightning appeared inside of it. Honey took Mathew's hand.

"Last chance to turn back."

"Let's just go and get this over with."

"Whatever happens, do not let go of my hand."

They stepped through the portal together, and it vanished behind them. The room stood empty and silent for five seconds, and Mathew reappeared in a flash of purple light. His face gaunt and pale, he was curled up in the fetal position on the floor. Sweat covered him, and his eyes were wide with a stare that seemed to see nothing but go on forever.

A moment later the witch reappeared with another flash. "I did warn you," she said. "Still, I have to admit, the neighborhood beautification program the new chaos god has been enacting has really yielded some positive results. The street signs aren't exactly useful in a place where direction and time are both meaningless, but it did make it feel more, homey.

"Still, you did very well. Five whole seconds and you kept your sanity. I've got to hand it to you, you're much stronger willed than I gave you credit for. I am sorry about your pants. I could only save one thing and I had to make a choice. I know pinky toes aren't the most important of appendages, but I thought, 'Pants are replaceable'. You signed the waver, however, so not really my responsibility.

"Anyway, I hope you were able to tell through all the spatial distortion that everyone there was trying to dress like me. Except that one bitch, but don't even get me started on Melissa. Look at me going on and on when I should really hide you before Alma sees you. I do hope you're able to move again when it's time to leave. I'd hate for the trip to be delayed. Don't worry, I'll take care of you until then. One last thing, and I'll deny it if you ever claim I said this, but you have nice butt."

Chapter 12

Alma, Mathew, Alteem, and Honey stood outside of their home's door. They had backpacks with bedrolls attached to the top, except Honey, who just had her bag.

"Are you sure you're okay?" Alma asked.

"I'm fine," said Mathew.

"It's just I haven't seen you all week, and now you look a little distraught."

"I've just been feeling a little under the weather."

"If you're sure your fine."

"I'm fine mother, really."

Honey chirped in, "Are we all ready to go?"

"Yes dear, I think we are," said Alma.

"It'll be alright," Alteem assured Alma.

The four set out walking on the road. They walked for half a day when Alma stopped on the road.

"What's wrong?" Alteem asked her.

"This is it," Alma said. "One more step and it will be the furthest I've ever been away from my home.

"It's okay, Mom," said Mathew. "We're right here with you."

"How could you possibly know that?" asked Honey.

"I just, it's just as far as I've ever gone before."

"In this specific direction? Or in all directions? Did you measure out the mileage then check to make sure?"

"No, I didn't do that."

"Then how do you know? I could understand if it was a building, or a landmark, or even the end of a field or something, but we're just in the middle of the road."

"I guess I don't know for sure, but this is definitely as far as I've been in this direction."

"Why here then? Why did you just walk to this nowhere place, mark it down so you'd remember it, and turn back?"

"I just, came this far and got nervous, ok."

"I don't know, still seems a little iffy to me."

"It was in this general area."

"What's with the one more step thing then?"

"It's an emotional moment for me, I'm sorry its troubling you so much."

"Take it from someone who's been everywhere. No patch of earth is more important than any other, it's all just a bunch of rock, dirt, and sand."

"This is my home, and I'm leaving it for the first time ever. You had a home you had to leave once didn't you. All the homes you destroyed might not have meant much to you, but those buildings and streets carried memories in them. Lives had been lived there, and even if many of them have been wiped away by your indifferent magic, it all still happened. There were lifetimes of laughter and tears, however small they may seem to you. So one patch of dirt is not the same as any other, for people might have fallen in love on some of those patches. Others were born or died there. Even once it's all gone, it still means something, and this is my patch of earth. My parents died here, my son was born here, this was the last place I saw my first husband alive, and this as far as I've ever been from it."

"Give or take."

"Yes, give or take. I should point out," Alma continued. "It's also where I met Alteem, where I met you, and where *you* met me. You've definitely changed my world, and to what end, none can yet see. I think we've changed yours too, doesn't that mean something to you."

The witch glanced around with a sheepish look in her eyes. "Maybe."

"Why not help me along, as we leave *our* home?" Alma held out her hand to Honey.

Honey placed her own hand inside of Alma's, and she felt her squeeze it.

"Let's go," said Alma, and they began walking again.

The party travelled eastward first, to the eastern coast of the peninsula. The great ports there made for easier roads and travel. Though many had diminished or been abandoned, like all else, they were beginning to come back.

The coast was mostly cliffs, with ports only built along the lower sections. The larger cities had far more abandoned buildings than the smaller ones. It made places somewhat creepy when half the buildings were going unused. Not even squatters or vandals could get around to them, there was so many. Sometimes an unusually ambitious vandal might try and deface them all, but inevitably it turned into too much of a task. What was the use of vandalizing something, if no one was going to care anyway?

The group mostly stayed in these places. While economies were recovering on the whole, it was somewhat difficult to run an inn when there was free real estate everywhere. The kings and owners might have had something to say about it, but they were all dead. As it turned out, people got along just fine without them. Some people did worry about someone raising an army and trying to come along to conquer them and insist maybe they did need a ruler, but others just argued there was no need to willingly let someone be their master now just because someone might come along to force them to do it later.

The real problem was roads, specifically paved roads. Dirt roads did a fine job of forming themselves. All you really had to do to get a dirt road was keep going along the same way, once enough people do it, you had a nice, flat-ish, dirt road. It didn't work as well in places without dirt, but, fortunately, dirt was fairly abundant. Paved roads were beginning to fall into disrepair. The one thing governments were really good at, or at least, capable of, or, you know, could do, was make and maintain paved roads. Sometimes bridges too, but bridges are really just a method of connecting roads together.

In the witches time she'd gotten around to repairing a good deal of roads. Once she was gone, her government quickly fell apart. Most roads remained in poor condition.

Local councils, of course, cropped up all over the place, but they were mostly concerned with ineffective neighborhood watches and restricting the colors people could paint their houses. Protecting property values might seem like a pointless exercise in a world with so much free property, but it was something people really cared about.

Governments are also quite good at fighting wars. That's not true, they're not good at it, but if human history is any indication, they are quite fond of doing so. So much so that it begs the question if the only reason they bother to build roads is so they can fight wars that much faster. This governmental obsession was the problem that had led the group to embark on their journey. Not building roads, but that people were forming governments again and those governments were much more eager to get to warring than to road building.

Many had speculated why it was governments liked to war so much. The chief reason seemed to be so that they could acquire more territory. More territory meant they would have more people and resources. More people and more resources meant they would be better at fighting wars. More territory also meant they would have more roads to build and maintain, but it was worth it for better wars. The great question remains, will governments one day care more about building roads than fighting wars?

They were less than a week into their journey when they saw a group of people coming in the opposite direction from them. As they grew closer they noticed the group wasn't traveling along the road so much as it was fleeing in horror.

Standing to the side as the group rushed past them, Alteem managed to grab one of the calm ones(calm being a relative term in this case). "What happened?"

"It was..." the man started, but his words trailed off as he seemed to remember. "No, I cannot think of it, a beast, a monster, a terror. It came out of the sea and attacked the city. Most fled, some were frozen in fear and...nothing can stop such a beast. This is the end times. Flee, flee while you can."

Alteem turned to his party. "We have to do something."

"What?" Asked Alma.

"Fight it, kill it."

"Mother can't fight such a thing," said Mathew.

"I'll take Honey, we can fight it together." Said Alteem.

"You're getting to old to play the hero." Said Alma.

"Honey will be with me, whatever creature waits for us, it cannot be more frightening than her."

"Be careful."

"So," said Honey. "No one's going to ask if I even want to go?"

"Honey, will you please come with me to stop an unknown horror and save countless lives in the process?" Asked Alteem.

Honey dithered for a moment. "I suppose, but only because you said that nice thing about how frightening I am."

"Let's be off then, the faster we move the more lives might be saved."

Alma hugged and kissed Alteem before they left. They set as a fast a pace as Alteem could manage. It still took near an hour before they saw it. It appeared first on the horizon, gargantuan in size, it rivaled mountains. The creature moved slowly, buildings being crushed as it slithered this way and that. It wasn't until they got closer they could better make out its form.

The creature was a mass of tentacles, some small and wriggling, others thicker than trees and writhing always. Gaps would appear as the tentacles wormed around and from between them eyes would pear out in all directions. Even in glimpses the eyes looked huge, and would bulge out from the gaps before the tentacles swarmed around them again. At times, instead of eyes, a mouth would appear. Some of the mouths had long pointed teeth that yawned open and stretched out. Others were shark like and round, with rows of teeth puckering together. The worst of all were the ones that looked human and were smiling with perfectly white teeth.

The abomination would stretch out several tentacles and rip buildings off of the ground. It tore them apart, and Alteem only figured out what it was doing when it found a hiding survivor in one of homes. It lifted the poor soul out of its hiding place and dropped him into its body where he quickly disappeared to what was surely a horrible fate.

Alteem froze in place as he watched it. It could have easily crushed the city, but it was making a game of rooting around building by building. His senses came back to him and he broke into a run, hoping to reach the creature before it found any more survivors. He stopped when he realized Honey wasn't with him.

Turning around he saw her standing looking at a creature the way a person would look at a face they couldn't quite remember but knew they knew. Then recognition finally dawned and she spoke.

"Is that Georgie?" she said. Standing on her toes she began to wave frantically. "Georgie! Georgie! It's me Honeydrops."

Alteem looked back at the creature. It grew stiff as she called out to it, somehow hearing her across the distance. It dropped the building it was holding which splintered apart as it hit the ground. It slithered across the ground towards, them, covering so much distance in such a short time Alteem fell back as it loomed before them seconds later. It dug up earth as it moved and the ocean rushed in behind it.

An eye appeared on the body and stretched out with the tentacles until it was only a few feet away from her. A voice that sounded like several people gasping for breath emerged from the creature. "Honeydrops? I don't believe it, it's really you. I didn't know this planet is where you were from."

"I almost didn't recognize you at first," said Honey. "You've grown so big."

"Yes, I really should go on a diet, I've been meaning to for a while now. I really don't know how you manage to keep your figure."

"Gorging on an entire city probably isn't helping you any," Honey laughed.

"I know, I know."

"Oh, this is my friend, Alteem."

The eye turned to regard him, "Hey, how's it going?" It asked before turning back to Honey.

"So what are you doing here?" Honey asked.

"You know how it is, some group of cultist summoned me thinking I would grant them ultimate power."

"Let me guess, you ate them."

"You know me to well. You'd think these silly humans would learn. All the evidence points to it being a bad idea, but they think they know better. What have you been up to lately?"

"Well, first off, I conquered the world."

"Good for you, you had a dream and you accomplished it. You know, everybody always talks about doing these things, but you actually did it."

"Here's the thing though, I always thought ruling the world would make be happy, but it was nothing but trouble."

"Nooooo."

"Yes, I had control over everybody, but no control over my life. And you know what, you can't make people love you. I tried, boy, did I try, but in the end it just doesn't work. I don't even know if it was really my dream, or if it is was my Mother's dream for me. Long story short, I swore evil off and I'm good now."

"What, say it isn't so. You were the last person I would have imagined turning good."

"I wasn't happy Georgie."

"Are you happy now?"

"I'm not quite there yet, but I'm happier."

"I gotta be honest, I don't know what to think about all this."

"What about you? Are you happy?"

"Wow, no one's ever asked me that before."

"I'm asking you now, are you happy?"

"I really get a great deal of pleasure out of being evil."

"Sure, who doesn't, but are you happy?"

"I mean, what is happiness really?"

"It's a simple question Georgie."

"I don't know what to say to you right now."

"But doesn't that say everything? Seems to me if you were happy you'd be able to say it."

"Maybe your right, but what am I supposed to do about it?"

"I don't know Georgie, I think we all have to find our own answer to that question."

"Seems like I've got a lot of thinking to do."

"That's good though, it took me months to just, look inside and think. I still haven't completely found my way, but I feel like I'm at least on my way."

"I'm really glad I ran into you."

"Me too, we really shouldn't go this long without seeing each other."

"Yeah, definitely, stop by and visit any time."

"I will."

"Could I possibly get a ride home from you?"

"Of course," Honey held up her hands and began to swirl them around each other. A swirling gateway of purple lightning appeared and began to suck in Georgie like spaghetti. It took some time given the size of it, but once the portal disappeared the creature was gone.

"I think," said Honey. "The day, is saved. And I got to help out a friend. Being good feels nice. I suppose we should get back, right Alteem? Alteem?"

Alteem still sat on the ground, staring at Honey. The witch started to look around, feeling awkward as he looked at her for several minutes. Then at last he spoke, "What the fuck just happened?"

Chapter 14

Alteem and Honey were walking back to their party, "Your name is Honeydrops, and that things name is Georgie," said Alteem

"That's just my nickname for him. You can't really pronounce its name with the human tongue, but it's something like G'eo'rg'eea. Georgie is just easier to say."

"What was it?"

"There's not really a word for them. They're creatures born from the abyss between realities."

"You mean, there's more than one of those things?"

"Yeah, but, they're all different. You should see Georgie's girlfriend, or maybe boyfriend...partner. Difficult to describe really since it's not so much a body as a...imagine bloody diarrhea mixed with vomit as a sort of chunky mist. Fortunately, nobody has to see it long since it dissolves people. I have magic that protects me...it's more the smell really."

"Are they a species?"

"That's not the right word. There's a specific criteria for what makes a species. They're more a kind of creature. A 'kind' doesn't mean anything."

"How do you know that thing?"

"How does one ever meet anybody? You meet people, they introduce you to other people. It just happens. I've palled around with some demons in my youth and we had some crazy times together. The sorts of things you meet when you're hanging out with demons aren't the same sort of things you're going to run into when you hang out with princes or farmers."

"Palled around with demons?"

"When you spend all your time studying ancient magics in a swamp with an oppressive mother you take what friends you can get. Of course there was Hredellenar, the demon prince. He was very fond of me, and if I'm being honest, I was fond of him too. He proposed, but I turned him down. I'd heard about demon-human hybrid births and none of them work out well for the mother."

"Demons were your friends?"

"If demons are the only people who will be your friends, then you find yourself friends with demons."

"Do you miss them?"

The witch cocked her head to the side thinking about it, "They were never very nice."

"Would you expect demons to behave differently?"

"I don't want to stereotype."

"I think you can stereotype demons."

"That's very small minded of you Alty."

"They're demons." Alteem said, looking at Honey from the side of his eye.

"How many demons have you known?"

"Not many, thankfully."

"This is a very ugly side of you." Honey put a little more distance between the two of them.

"If there is one group that's okay to judge, it's demons. You already said they weren't nice."

"I hung out with a rough crowd. It's not like nice and good are the same thing."

"Are you saying there was good demons?"

"Some were, *less* evil."

"Less evil is still evil."

"What do you expect, they literally grew up in hell. That's the sort of environment that's going to be really tough on a kid."

"Demons will always be demons."

"I've certainly learned something about you today, and I don't like it very much." Honey crossed her arms and looked away from Alteem.

"Don't make me out to be a bad guy here. I'm justified in hating demons."

"It's not like most humans have ever been nicer to me than demons."

"That's because you killed their families, burned their homes, and enslaved them."

"As if they would have accepted me even if I hadn't done those things. With my powers, with how different I am, I was always destined to be hated and feared. At least it was on my terms."

Honey's face had grown dark, and Alteem suddenly worried about what he should say next. She was right, he knew, it was always going to be her fate to be hated and feared. No matter how hard she tried she wasn't going to change that. Despite this, he did not want her to abandon the path she was one.

"Why am I even doing this?" she asked.

"So that you don't hate yourself, even if you can't make others stop. I was a prince, remember, I too know what it is to be hated and feared. Not as much as you, but it was as inevitable for me as for any witch. I had the bonus of also being loved and adored by some. Ernloheim was a hard land, and things were not always easy. Some things were done because they had to be done. I always did my best to act with honor, not because it meant people wouldn't hate me. I did it so I wouldn't hate myself, or, to just hate myself less. It was the best I could hope for sometimes."

"You don't care about me." Honey said.

"I care about the person you're trying to be. I care about the path you're on. Not just because I fear what you might do should you leave it, but because I also need to believe people can come back from the darkest of places. Maybe it's not true, but I need to believe no matter how long the journey, we can all come back. You *and* me."

"What if I can't?"

"I don't have anywhere near your burden to bear, but I still haven't made it back myself. Perhaps there is no end. Even if I knew the journey to redemption was endless, I'd keep walking it."

"Forever is very long time."

"The longest of times."

Honey looked up at him, and met his eyes. Alteem thought he might be seeing her for the first time. She put up so many walls that it was hard to know who the real person was underneath them. Here she was now, small, frail and lost.

"Forever then." She said.

Alteem nodded.

Chapter 15

The party of four huddled together as the afternoon was wearing on. Dark clouds approached and threatened to rain.

"There's several towns nearby, it would be nice to sleep in one of them rather than camping outside," said Alteem. "Perhaps Bandleford.

"Not Bandleford," said the witch.

"Why not?"

"Because I've been there before."

"Gargaville?"

"No."

"Stenelfell?"

"No."

"Cranston?"

"I don't remember any Cranston."

"Cranston it is then."

The party of four then headed towards Cranston. They arrived as evening was approaching. One of the villagers looked up at them as they approached. His eyes squinted.

"Gods help us!" He shouted. "It's the witch, she's returned. She'll kill us all." The man fled, screaming as he went. Others heard his cry and took up cries of their own. It did not take long before the whole village was fleeing in panic and terror.

The witch snapped her fingers, "Now I remember Cranston."

Later, the party sat around its campfire. The starless night had greeted them with a light drizzle. But for Honey's magic, they might not have been able to get a fire going at all.

"We need a disguise for Honey." Said Mathew.

"Agreed," said Alteem.

"What for?" said Honey.

"That's the third day in a row people have run screaming at the sight of you."

"I was in a particularly prolific mood when I first arrived in this region."

"I'll go into a village tomorrow and see if I can't get some clothes for her." Said Alma.

"Silk please," said Honey.

"The plainer the better," said Alteem.

"I have never in my life worn plain clothes. This is an atrocity."

"You've committed much worse atrocities in your lifetime."

"Name one."

"Slaughtering most of the planet's population."

"...Name two."

"Poisoning the land causing starvation and sickness in untold numbers."

Honey glared at Alteem who stared right back at her. "Name thr-"

"You're wearing the clothes!"

Honey pouted. "You don't have to yell."

Not much of the next day had passed when Alma returned with the clothes, a plain green dress with a white undershirt and a dark green scarf to cover up her hair.

"I'm doing this under protest." Said Honey.

"I know," said Alteem. "We all know."

The witch snatched the clothes out of Alma's hands and started to strip.

"Go change out of sight."

Marching off, the witch mumbled insults under her breath. She returned in her new clothes. Still beautiful, her effect was diminished without her lavish outfits. She looked much younger as well, though no more timid with her face twisted in anger. Her mismatched eyes were the only clue to her true identity. Alteem did not doubt people would stare at Honey's eyes, but he doubted anyone would realize who she was. People might have found her gaze unsettling, but few knew why.

She summoned a mirror and her anger melted away into distress as she examined herself. "I look...I look...ordinary."

"No, you don't," said Alma. "Maybe we should smudge some dirt on her face to make her less pretty. As it is, I think people will stare at her more this way. We don't need every boy from here to our destination stopping us to hit on her."

"No please," Honey fell to her knees and gripped the hem of Alma's skirt. "You've taken away my beautiful clothes, don't take away my beautiful face."

Alma laughed, "Only teasing you dear."

"I knew that," the witch said, jumping to her feet and brushing off her dress.

The party hit the road again the next day. The witch moaning and sighing as they walked. Her mood improved as everyone they passed smiled at them, and her in particular. "You're very pretty," some of them said to her. "I know," she'd say back.

"I don't understand," Honey said. "Everyone is so much nicer to me in this much uglier dress."

"It's not the dress." Said Alteem

"What else could it be?"

"It's because they don't instantly recognize you as someone who killed someone or many someone's they cared about."

"Are you sure it's not the dress?"

"Yes."

"On a scale of one to ten how sure are you?"

"Ten."

"That's really sure." Honey sunk deep into thought. Tempting as it was for them to ask her what she was thinking about, they were all much too happy to not have her whine anymore. Days past, then a full week, and finally Mathew cracked.

"What are you thinking about?"

"I was just weighing how much I like people being nice to me over how much I like my old clothes."

"For a week?"

"I really like my clothes, besides, they're only nice to me because they don't know who I am. Sure I could completely redesign my look, maybe go for a whole good witch thing, adopt a new persona. Even then, it wouldn't be me they liked. Is it worth being someone else to feel loved if it's not really you that's being loved?"

Everyone exchanged glances, "I don't know." Alma said eventually. "That's not a question someone else can answer for you."

"She could try it," said Alteem. "It would be good for us if she was pretending to be someone else."

"Would it be 'good', Alteem?"

Alteem said nothing in response.

"It's up to you, Honey, if you want to try it." Alma said.

"Then, from now on," said Honey. "I am the good witch...Kay...Tee. How am I doing so far?"

"You're doing great." Said Alma

"That's a relief, I've never been a good witch before. It's exhausting."

They made camp for the evening, and Honey disappeared into one of her temporary dimensions to redo her look. When she emerged she was wearing a green gown with tiny golden leaves embroidered along the shoulders, curling around the arms and turning to thorns along the sleeves. A scarf like autumn leaves was wrapped around her head to cover her hair. A belt that looked like wheat braided together wrapped around her waist and trailed down her side nearly a foot. Around the skirt of the gown were brown trees with leaves of orange and red falling continuingly off of them.

"So," Honey said. "What do you think?"

"We're trying not to stand out," said Alteem.

"I know, that's why it's so subtle."

"I think people are less likely to recognize her this way," said Mathew.

"Maybe you're right," said Alteem.

"Is that all anyone has to say, it's not like dress making magic is easy," said Honey.

"You use magic to make your dresses?" asked Mathew.

"They don't form naturally out of the air, it would take someone years to make something like this by hand. Also, you know, the falling leaves thing at the bottom. That's not possible by natural means."

"Just to be clear, your magical training growing up included how to destroy all life on earth, and dress making."

"And magic cake baking, but that hasn't much come in handy yet."

"Why?"

"Who doesn't like cake?"

"I meant why did you learn that?"

"I hoped once I conquered the world there would be parties, you can't have a party without a cake."

"People have parties without cakes all the time."

"Really? I don't have much experience with parties. I threw one once I conquered the world, but my army just got drunk and started fighting each other. No one even touched the cake."

"And after you went to all that effort." Mathew said.

"I know, thank you."

"I'm going to bed."

"So no one's got anything to say about my dress?"

"Are you going to sleep in it?" asked Alma.

"I...I'd better change back into the peasant clothes for the night."

Honey returned to her new outfit when they hit the road again in the morning. Less people called her pretty, but a great many more stared at her. The witch believed it was in admiration.

On the road they arrived at a small city called Tellerston. They weren't far into the city when cries arose that a fire was spreading in a part of the city. The party rushed to find several buildings already ablaze. The flames roaring as the people formed a useless bucket line to pour water on it.

Honey raised her open hand, and closed it. Within less than a second the fire vanished, not even leaving embers behind. The front of the bucket line stopped, with a few buckets further back still moving before they too realized what had happened. People looked around, trying to figure out what just happened when they spotted the woman dressed like no normal person would, her hand still raised up. She lowered her hand suddenly looking nervous.

A man stepped forward out of the crowd. "You stopped the fire?"

"Since I was here," Honey shrugged.

"You're a witch."

"I'm a good witch, the good witch Kaytee."

"Where have you been, what happened to all of you?"

Honey paused for a moment, opening her mouth several times but not saying anything. "There's a really good reason I haven't been around, but I can't tell it to you right now. Oh, wait, no, I thought of one. I had to hide, because of Honeydrops, but now that she's gone, we good witches can come out of hiding again."

"Who's Honeydrops?"

"The...evil witch who conquered the entire world."

"Seriously, that's her name?"

"She didn't want people to know her real name," Honey frowned at herself.

"I can see why, it's a silly name."

"It's a little silly, but it's not that silly."

"It's pretty silly on its own, but for someone who spread a, less eternal than previously believed, darkness across the land, it's downright bizarre."

"I think maybe you're making this out to be more than it really is. It's just a name right? You should probably just forget that's her name and definitely not tell anybody about it."

"Honeydrops? I'm gonna be lying awake tonight thinking about that. She was so evil and that's her name."

"Was she really that evil?" Honey asked.

"Yes." The villager said, several others nodding along with him.

"She did a lot of bad things I admit, but maybe she was just on a bad direction in her life and needed some perspective."

"Perspective? I don't care what she did towards the end of her rule, she was irredeemable."

"You think? Irredeemable?"

"We should keep moving," Alteem said, putting a hand on her shoulder.

"Won't you stay the night," said the man. "You probably saved half the city the way that fire was spreading. We should celebrate your arrival."

"Celebrate?" Honey said, hope in her eyes as she turned to Alteem.

"Time is of the essence," said Alteem and started walking.

"Phooey," said the witch. "At least I'm two for two on saving the day."

They continued on their journey through the town, and across the landscape. Along the way Honey managed to resolve several crisis in the towns, villages, and cities they came across. She opened up a collapsed mine saving several trapped people inside. She stopped a locust swarm that threatened to consume fields of crops. She blocked water from a broken dam that threatened to destroy several towns along the river below, then she repaired the dam. At one town she ran into an old demon friend of hers who had possessed a small girl. After a short chat she convinced him to leave.

"I'm not used to traveling," Said Alma. The group had stopped by a roadside inn for the night and were sitting down together at a table. "Is it normal to run into so many crisis?"

"I was wondering that too," said Honey. "It does seem unusual that everywhere we go there's some crisis that crops up that we can easily solve within a short time frame and then be on our way. I thought maybe the reason it seemed so strange to me is because in all my past traveling I was the crisis."

"It's definitely unusual," said Mathew. "I don't think I've ever encountered a region with so many troubles. Sure everywhere has its problems, but they're usually systemic economic and cultural problems that can't be solved so easily. Sometimes there's raiders, but that hasn't been as big of a problem since you fell out of power."

"I was voluntarily deposed."

"Then of course you have small feuds between families, the occasional bandit, too many orphans can be problem since you killed so many children's parents."

"It's not like I spared the children on purpose, but they're small, they can hide easier. I killed them whenever I could." Honey paused and smoothed her dress. "A thing for which I am now deeply sorry."

"And of course, weather disasters."

"I don't know what you're talking about," said Alteem. "It was always like this whenever I traveled as a prince."

"It can't have always been like this," said Mathew.

Alteem shrugged.

Everyone went silent for a brief moment.

"When you make the magic cake," said Alma. "Do you make it out of nothing, or do you need ingredients?"

"They don't require ingredients so much as reagents, which most summoning spells do require."

"You summon the cakes?"

"It's more of a conjuration, but the fundamentals are the same."

"Is it just one type of cake, or do you have different flavors?"

"Much like real cake I can make a cake in just about any flavor, that doesn't mean it will taste good. There are a few more magical flavors that would be difficult to make a normal cake with."

"Like what?"

"Nether matter, starlight, the souls of the damned."

"What do the souls of the damned taste like?"

"Lemony."

"Really?"

"Yes, but not in a good way. It's like, too little lemon, so it's mostly bland and stale. Plus you have nightmares for a week after eating it, so it's not worth it all, and, you know, it's all empty calories."

"What about the other two?"

"Starlight is nice, like a sweet and spicy vanilla flavor. Nether matter is completely tasteless. Which is strange when you think about the fact that everything has a taste, so it's interesting to eat for the novelty, but not something you need to eat more than once."

"And the dress making, is that conjuration?"

"It's more like magical weaving, there are magical flows in the world and I take them and spin them into a material. Then I use my magic to turn it into a dress. I prefer a combination of nether matter and laughter. It's very soft, see, feel."

Alma reached over to feel Honey's dress. "Wow, that is very soft, laughter you say."

"Sure, there's magic in everything, it's just a matter of how strong that magic is. You can make a dress out of just about anything, cake too really. It's all a matter of how well it comes out. Some things are more suited than others for such things."

"How do you do magic?"

"There's another sense you have develop over time. It's like seeing into a different world, but it's different than normal sight, the same way seeing is different than hearing."

"How hard is it?"

"Takes practice, and going too fast can have some terrible consequences."

"Like what?"

"Oh, death, destruction, spawning abominations, or, worst of all, permanently changing your own hair color."

"Can't you just dye it?"

"I could for a time, but there's so much magic flowing through me now that it just overrides the dye."

"Can't you just use the magic to change it back?"

"I tried...once."

"What happened?"

Honey didn't say anything, her gaze became distant, and she took a sip from her cup.

"Could you teach someone magic?"

"I never have before. We're not really supposed to share our secrets with people outside of our coven."

"Would you teach someone magic, if they asked?"

"No one's ever asked before, I don't have the best reputation."

"Why do you want to learn magic mother?" Asked Mathew. "And from her."

"Is that what you were getting at?" Honey asked.

"If you can make cakes from starlight, and grow forests, it might be nice to see if a person could have magical garden. Imagine it, a garden of starlight." Said Alma.

"Not very ambitious," said Honey. "But my ambitions didn't go so well so maybe that's not such a bad thing. Alright! You're officially my apprentice."

"Are you sure I'm not too old to start learning magic?"

"You are definitely too old to start learning magic. But you've been kind to me, in a world where no one else was willing to be kind to me. And I don't deserve any kindness. If it's not too late for me, then it's not too late for anyone. I am the greatest witch who ever lived, if anyone can find a faster way to teach someone magic, I can."

Chapter 16

Alma and Honey sat apart from the others just off the road. A few trees were scattered about them as the morning light shown down warmly above them.

"Lesson one of magic: Reality is your bitch," said Honey.

"I'm not sure I understand," said Alma.

"It's all about attitude. You need to think of everything as beneath you. The very fabric of all things is less than you are. Become ultimate, the greatest thing in existence, be it baby."

"I don't think everything is beneath me."

"Start."

"Isn't there a gentler more subtle way to do magic?"

"It's not as fun."

"It might be more, me."

"If that's really the way you want to do it."

"Please."

"I guess...for you...go ahead and sit against that tree."

"Okay," said Alma. Carefully lowering herself so she sat with her back against the nearest tree.

"The tree breathes, and as all the trees of the world breathe, so breathes the planet. Feel the tree breathe. So slow it's hard to perceive, but it breathes. When you feel the tree breathe you can begin to feel the world breathe. Then there's the sun in the sky, which breathes a single breathe in its lifetime. Spewing forth matter from its stellar furnace before it finally gives way, and breathes back in, collapsing into darkness. It is a single star among trillions of stars in the galaxy. Each breathing one single breathe across their lifespans. Our galaxy is just one galaxy among countless galaxy. The universe breathes as stars are born and die. Who knows how many breathes may happen across time and space. Our universe is just one universe among endless universes. Each one breathing as they come to being and slowly die out. Each one with its own dimensions and layers of reality. Inside that breath, the breath of the cosmos, you can feel the interconnected stream of being. Feel it across the unimaginable breadth of all things. When you can feel that, changing reality at will is a simple thing. Tell me Alma, what do you feel?"

"I feel comfortable," said Alma. "I wouldn't have thought it, but sitting against a tree is surprisingly cozy."

"I know, right? You think bark would be stiff and ruff, but it's very nice."

"Yeah, you just fit right into it. It's like trees are perfect for people to sit against."

"So true, so true, you have a spider on your shoulder."

Alma looked at the spider on her shoulder. Under other circumstances she might have been more startled, but she was feeling calm sitting against the tree, so she just flicked it off.

"What about the breath of the cosmos and the interconnectedness of all things?" asked Honey.

"None of that."

"That's okay, it normally takes a couple of decades of meditating on it."

"You really think I can do this?"

"Of course you can, just give me time to come up with some ways to speed up the process. For now just, meditate harder."

"Okay..." Alma said, settling back into the tree.

Honey stood there for a few seconds, watching Alma. "Time's up for today. Alteem says we need to get back on the road."

"Already?"

"We only had a few minutes. Maybe if we got a cart you could mediate while we're on the road. Problem is there's no trees on carts. Do carts breathe? No. We'll get a potted plant for you to hold."

"Won't we need a horse to pull the cart?"

"Nah, I'll just magic something up."

Honey helped Alma to her feet and they joined Alteem and Mathew.

"How did it go?" Asked Alteem.

"Not much progress today," said Honey. "But I'm feeling optimistic. We're going to get a cart at the next town, and a potted plant."

"Won't we need a horse for that?" Asked Mathew.

"We have a witch," said Honey. "Soon we'll have two."

"How joyful." Said Mathew.

"It's great, I know."

"Do you not pick up on my sarcasm or do you deliberately ignore it?"

"I ignore it."

"I still don't understand why you want to do this, Mother." Mathew said to Alma.

"I always thought magic was destruction," Said Alma. "Terror, conjuring storms and such."

"You don't want to throw fireballs and shoot lightning out of your hands?" Asked Honey.

"I'm sure such things are useful if you want to slay monsters or conquer the world, but what would I do with that?"

"I can conjure earthquakes too."

"And what good does that do you now?"

Honey thought for a moment. "It might be a cool effect at a dance party, if I keep it small."

"If magic can make dresses and cake, maybe I could use magic to find a way to wash clothes."

"Wash clothes?" Mathew said in disbelief. "You want to master the hidden forces of the universe to wash clothes?"

"Do you have any idea how many hours in my life I have spent washing clothes? If I could just magic it away I would have so much time to do the things I've always wanted. How much time I could save, *every* woman could save, if I could make magic washing machines. Imagine magically run farms. Look at the labor across the world that goes into growing food. If it could all be done by magic it would change everything. Honey grew an entire forest in a day. Think of a field of crops that harvests itself, a world without hunger. That's just the beginning, if magic can do anything, then we can find a way for magic to do everything. Then *we* can do everything and anything."

"What if I used an earthquake to...no nevermind." Said Honey.

"That's brilliant, Mother." Said Mathew.

"You got your brilliance from somewhere, Mathew." Said Alteem.

"Just peasant things," said Alma.

"There's got to be at least one useful thing an earthquake can be used for." Said Honey. "Demolition!"

"Demolition needs to be controlled for it to be safe." Said Mathew.

"Damn it."

"We should get moving," said Alteem.

Once more, the party set out on the road, traveling through the day until they reached the next village. It was not at all surprising anymore, when they approached and saw people fleeing in terror.

"This is really normal for you?" asked Mathew.

"Always happened everywhere I went." Alteem said. "Let's go see what's going on."

"It's the goatmen!" Someone shouted. "They're raiding the village!"

"Filthy animals," Alteem cursed.

"They're actually nice enough once you get to know them." Said Honey.

"I'm not interested in getting to know them." Alteem reached for a sword that hadn't been there in many years. "Let's go, we need to save these people." He grabbed the witches hand and rushed into the village.

A group of near twenty goatmen were running through the village, ransacking food supplies, burning houses, and cutting down anyone who got in there way.

"Hey," said the witch. The goatmen stopped, all turning to look at her. "Stop it." A goatman raised an ax to split someone's head in two. "No," said Honey, and the goatman hesitated. "Put it down. I said. Put. It. Down." The goatman dropped his ax.

"What are you doing?" asked Alteem.

"I don't know, I just always talked to the goatman this way and they responded to it. It's how I got them to serve in my army."

"That cannot be true."

"All of you now, gather round, good, good, now sit. That means all of you, I see you back there." The last remaining goatmen sat down in front of Honey. "All of you listen, no more killing people. No, not even a little. You're going to be good boys, or girls, whichever you are. Understood?"

The goatman all nodded.

"What clan are all of you?"

One of the creatures mumbled something.

"I can't understand you when you mumble, speak up."

"The doomhowl clan." The goatmen said.

"Where's your herd now?"

"They're up northwards."

"Okay, you there, you're going to take me and my friends to them. The rest of you are going to stay here and help fix all the damage you've done. You're not going to hurt anybody, or do anything bad. Do I make myself clear? I said, do I make myself clear!?"

They all mumbled.

"I don't want to repeat myself about the mumbling."

"Yes miss," they all said.

"Good, now let's go."

The goatman the witch pointed to got to his feet and started to lead the way. Stopping to look back when he noticed they weren't following.

"I don't believe this," Said Alteem. "This can't be real. The goatman have forever raided our villages, killed our people, burned our fields, and all we ever needed to do was talk to them with a firm hand."

Honey shrugged.

"I've gone insane, that's what it is. I'm still in the cell and none of this has been real. My mind must have snapped from having to constantly listen to you whine about your inane problems."

"That's hurtful," said Honey

"It's a joke, it's just the punchline of my own madness."

"I'd really like to be patient while you have your mental breakdown, but the sooner we get to the herd the sooner we can stop them from raiding anymore villages."

"Go then, doesn't matter, it's not real." Alteem dropped to his knees.

"You going to be okay if I leave you alone?"

"No, nothing is ever going to be okay. I'm never going to be okay."

"Okay, well, I'll see you when I get back."

The witch followed the Goatman, sparing a glance back for Alteem who was now pounding his fists against the floor.

Honey was a bit disappointed Alteem had remained behind. In order to get rid of the herd she'd have to convince the Kuuk, which was the title given to the leader of a herd. Not every herd had one, some herd just wandered aimlessly, following the first one of them to start walking in a direction each morning.

A goatman only rose to become a Kuuk when one of them managed to realize they could take over the herd simply by telling the others what to do. Once this happened, no one ever bothered to question it.

Since a raiding party had been sent away from the herd, it meant this herd must have a Kuuk. Groups never broke off from the herd without someone telling them to do so.

In the past Honey would have simply killed whoever was in charge of the goatman and then started issuing orders. Having forsworn evil, killing was unfortunately off the table. Violence might not be the answer, but it does provide a great deal of solutions. It meant she needed to come up with something to convince them. Kuuk's weren't as easy to boss around as other goatman.

"Who are you then?" Honey asked the Goatman.

"Veej Doomhowl." Said the Goatman.

Veej was the title given to warriors in the Goatman society, which was most of them.

"Can I just call you Frank, I'm gonna call you Frank."

"Frank Doomhowl?"

"No just Frank."

"What does Frank do?"

"Whatever you want, just don't hurt anyone."

"Whatever Frank want, Frank want to sit." The goatman sat down next to a tree. "Ooo, tree comfy."

"Yes, tree comfy, but you have to show me to the Herd."

"Frank not have to listen to no one, no more. Frank keep sitting."

Honey paused for a moment to think about that had just happened. "Shit." She said. The goatman thought that Frank was its new title. And when asking what the role of that title was, she'd given him permission to do as he pleased.

She slid down and next the goat, "Listen, I know you want to sit, but I'd really appreciate it if you showed me where you herd is."

"Frank not want to."

"Nice people help each other out."

"What you know about being nice?"

"I'm a good witch, we know all about being nice."

"Frank only knows one witch, and she not good. You look like her."

"We witches often look alike." Honey made sure her hair was covered.

"Frank can empathize, people often say we all look alike too. Frank show you where herd is."

"Thanks Frank you're a good guy, or possibly girl, whichever."

Frank got back to his or her feet and continued along the way. The sun was nearly gone by the time they finally arrived at the herd. Fires were lit, and Honey could smell meat charring. She knew the biggest fire would have the Kuuk.

"I can make my way from here Frank, you're a doll for showing me here."

"What you mean Frank doll?"

"It means, a person who is helpful."

"Colloquialism, Frank comprehend. You going to Kuuk Doomhowl?"

"Yes, I need to convince him to stop raiding and killing people."

"How else herd get food."

"There's lots of ways to get food. You could even offer services for money which can be exchanged for food."

"Services? Like interpretive dance?"

"I *love* interpretive dance. I once performed a twenty minute interpretive dance about my mother."

"Bad witch once make us watch twenty minute interpretive dance when we inside her army."

"What a strange coincidence." Honey glanced around "Did you like it?"

"Good dance, but many issues with mother, too many to dance away. Some problems even interpretive dance can't solve."

"So true, but in a perfect world it would solve everything."

"Maybe someday we make such world."

"Someday."

"Things not change, unless someone change them," Frank doll said, smacking a fist into his hand.

"Actually, everything is always in a state of flux and change, but I understand what you're getting at."

"No be so pedantic."

"Sorry."

Frank marched through the herd of goatmen. "Kuuk Doomhowl!" He or she roared upon approaching one of the goatmen.

"No need yell, Veej Doomhowl, me right here."

"Sorry, got over excited. Me no longer Veej Doomhowl, me now Frank."

"Frank Doomhowl? What Frank Doomhowl do?"

"Not Doomhowl either, Frank...Doll, and Frank Doll do whatever Frank Doll want so long as it doesn't hurt anyone."

"Kuuk Doomhowl no understand."

"Then Frank Doll help you understand, with dance." Frank began to dance, his or her body moving in the firelight. Large shadows danced with Frank in the moonlight. There was passion in the dance, and sweat and tears. The goatman moved, and the wind brushed across the flames sending them high into the air. For a moment the shadows became giants and Frank leapt into the air, finishing the dance.

Honey began clapping, but noticed she was the only one and stopped. "I thought it was good," she said, crossing her arms.

"Kuuk Doomhowl understand now." Said Kuuk Doomhowl. "Herd feel good, herd feel safe, easy to let others tell us where to go. Can't be wrong if we let others make all our decisions, but, can't be right either. No more Kuuks like me make all choices, time for us to start making right decisions, even if it means making wrong ones sometimes. Hear me Doomhowl, I am no longer Kuuk. I shall be, Deborah, Deborah Sandwich."

"Good name," said Frank Doll. "What you do, Deborah Sandwich?"

"Deborah has always wanted to be, a lumberjack."

"That okay, just make sure use sustainable methods."

Another Goatman stepped forward. "I shall be Tuesday Elfonso."

"And I," said another. "Shall be Stamina Warthog."

Soon the goatmen were all shouting their new names, and the Doomhowl herd was no more, except for the few who were still at the village. Also, a couple of other raiding parties were still out, but effectively, the Doomhowl herd was no more.

"We should celebrate this occasion," said Simon Roads. "With fire and food and dance."

"Good witch Kaytee, stay with us," said Frank Doll. "You showed us the way."

"I thought that was witch we used to work for," said Continental Apple.

"No, she good witch Kaytee now."

"You knew it was me the whole time," said Honey.

"Of course, have eyes," said Frank.

"And you don't hate me?"

"We followed you because that what we did, we followed. Always did we stand with you, never against. We as guilty as you, but if you be good, we can too."

"I really should go, we're kind of in a hurry."

Frank reached his or her hand out for the witch. "Dance one dance with me. New dance, for new future."

"I could stay for just one dance." Honey said taking Frank's hand.

Chapter 17

Alteem had not spoken much in the three days since the witch had been gone. Alma and Mathew did not know what was happening. When they'd arrived at the village he'd been spending a great deal of time staring at nothing. Attempts to get him to talk about what had happened produced no results.

Honey finally returned to the village, smiling and humming a pleasant tune.

"Where have you been?" Mathew asked.

"I just accidentally destroyed a millennia old social structure that's sure to have worldwide repercussions, what have you guys been up to?" Said Honey.

"Good repercussions or bad ones?"

"Good probably, I learned a lot about the Rodar, which is what the goatmen prefer to be called."

"I thought they didn't have a name for their own species." Said Mathew.

"Turns out no one's ever asked. We spent a lot of time dancing and talking, they were nice enough people before, but now that they've renounced evil they're downright lovely." Said Honey.

"You got them to renounce evil."

"Pretty much, yeah, plus I destroyed a repressive caste system. Like I said, it was mostly by accident, but I'm still putting it in the good deeds column. I decided it was time to leave once the orgy began. They invited me to join, and it has been a long time, but not *that* long."

"Orgy?"

"Not uncommon among the Rodar, as I learned. Once one of them gets horny they find the nearest willing partner and it's a domino effect from there. Gender doesn't even matter, it's just luck of the draw. Breeding is done by chance."

"How do they know who the father is then?"

"Doesn't matter, all Rodar children are considered family to everyone. It's all very progressive, especially now the raiding and murdering is over."

"How do they avoid incest if it's all random?"

"I hadn't thought of that, it is a bit gross isn't it. I suppose if you don't know it can't bother you." Honey shrugged.

"You're gross."

"I said I didn't join them. Okay, fine, maybe one handjob, but I just wanted to see how much bigger they were. You hear things, your curiosity gets peaked, you finally get your opportunity. I think you would have done the same in my position."

"No, I really wouldn't have." Said Mathew

"How are much bigger are they?" asked Alma.

"Mom!" Said Mathew.

"I'm not saying I would have done what she did, or that I approve, but since she already knows."

"Let's just say," said the witch. "If I'd have wanted to join the orgy, it would have been physically impossible for me to do so. And I lost my virginity to a demon."

"Are demons bigger too?"

"Mom, please stop." Said Mathew.

"They like to say so," said the witch. "But..."

"Isn't that always the case?" Said Alma.

"Not with the Rodar, as I just learned."

"Okay, I'm leaving," said Mathew, leaving.

"What's his problem?" Asked Honey.

"He's just uncomfortable hearing about this stuff from his mother." Said Alma.

"Penis sizes were probably twenty-five percent of what my mom talked to me about."

"That's, not normal."

"She was a real man's lady."

"Us non-witch folk have a different word for that sort of person."

"Soon enough you'll be witch folk, which reminds me, we need a cart, and a plant." Honey looked around. "The Rodan, there's still a few of them here. Hey! Hello! Gather round, you can stop repairing the town. That's right, go back to your herd. It's not really a herd anymore it's more of uh...you know what they'll dance it out for you. Good luck, bye." Honey waved at the Rodan as they headed back to their group. "Okay, cart time."

Honey looked around, and finding a suitable cart, used her magic to levitate it over. "Pity everyone fled in terror, it's not easy to locate a horticultural store." Honey disappeared into the town. Returning a few hours later, she had a bush nearly half her size floating beside her. "Look, I found a shrubbery."

"I think that's just a bush." Said Alma

"Well it was part of a shrubbery, plus it's more fun to say."

The bush/shrubbery floated over to the cart and set down gently inside. Honey walked over to Alteem who was sitting on the ground staring at other ground.

"Are we feeling better yet?" Asked Honey. "We need to get back on the road and all, you're the one who's always insisting on saving time." Alteem did not move nor speak. "Oh, you're impossible when you get in your moods."

"I've never seen him get into this sort of mood," said Alma.

"I did used to torture him and killed his family in front of him, it might have contributed. Okay, Alty, we need to get going so I'm just going to put you in the cart. If you object, groan or something."

Alteem remained silent.

"Alright then," Alteem was lifted of the ground with more purple magic and placed into the cart. "Okay, one cart, one shrubbery, and one Alteem. I think we're good to go. Mathew, we're leaving!"

Mathew came round a corner. "Are you done talking about penis sizes?"

"It's an ongoing conversation, but we've put it on hold for now. Help your mother onto the cart."

Mathew helped his mother onto the cart and followed her in.

"Now for a small bit of dark sorcery," said Honey, weaving her hands around each other. A swirling ball of purple lightning and wind funnels appeared in front of the cart, between the posts that normally held a horse. The ball grew until it nearly touched each post. After she ended her hand motions the ball remained in place, its energies swirling in a terrible vortex.

"Is that safe?" asked Mathew.

"Of course it's safe, just don't touch it. Unless you hate having hands, then go ahead and touch it." The witch waved her arms and the cart began to move forward. "Alma, sit next to the bush. Close your eyes, and remember, breath of the cosmos. And Alteem since you're sitting there too, if you feel like having any cosmos-y thoughts, go right ahead. Mathew, don't bother your mother."

The witch settled into the driver's seat of the cart, and kept the cart on track with her magic.

Chapter 18

"It's been a week," said Honey. "And every town and village we've seen has been abandoned."

"That is strange," said Mathew.

"Oh," Honey said, her hand moving to her mouth. "I know where we are. I didn't recognize it on account of everything not being covered in eternal darkness. We're in Ernloheim." Honey looked over to Alteem.

"Five days ago we crossed the border," he said.

"We should be coming up on it then," said the witch.

"On what?" asked Mathew.

It appeared over the horizon, the crystal palace of the witch. It did not glow so brightly with the sun shining down on it. The outline of it was not so stark in the blue sky, so it did not seem to claw at the sky anymore. The land around it was no longer a blackened ruin, but green and teeming with new life.

"Isn't it beautiful," said Honey.

"Well." Said Alma.

"Well?" Said Honey.

"Well..." Said Alma.

"Well!?" Said Honey.

"It might be, a little..."

"What?"

"Tacky." said Mathew.

"Gaudy," said Alma.

"Lurid."

"Garish."

"Ostentatious."

"I," the witch started to say something but stopped and paused before speaking again. "You're not seeing it right. The sun is ruining everything. And look at that field of flowers that started growing next to it, bleh. All this green, it's clashing with the colors. It wasn't designed for all this." She stood up on the cart. "Give me a second, I'll burn everything to the ground again."

"No," said Mathew, pulling her back to a seated position. "It won't help, Honey. Also just no."

"That was my masterpiece, my fortress of evil built to celebrate my victory in conquering the world. Everyone told me they loved it."

"They probably just said that because they were afraid of you killing them."

"No, but...but...Is that why my one woman shows always got standing ovations?"

"Listen, Honey," said Alma. "You've got a lot of talents. You're the most powerful witch in the world."

"What else am I not good at? Can I sing? Am I smart? Am I not pretty? What am I saying, of course I'm pretty. Holy shit, I planned the weddings of so many people, what if those were tacky too? Then there's all that financial advice I gave. All my cats kept dying but everyone insisted it wasn't my fault? Did anyone actually enjoy having sex with me? Do I care? Is it evil to be a selfish lover?"

"Please stop," said Mathew.

"Am I annoying? Everything is in question now. I always knew I wasn't a good person but this, where do I even start figuring this out. Quick, someone have sex with me."

"We're not having sex with you." Said Mathew.

The witch pulled up her knees and hugged them, rocking back and forth.

"What's the matter, Honey?" Asked Alma.

"No one's ever refused to have sex with me before." Said Honey, her voice verging on tears. "It's all been a lie."

Alma slid over on the cart to sit next to Honey and placed a hand on her shoulder.

"Thank you, Alma," The witch said leaning towards Alma to kiss her and starting to lift of her own dress..

"No." Said Alma.

The witch let her dress drop back down.

"I know, Honey, that learning everything you once thought was true is a lie, can be difficult, but it's just part of growing up."

"I'm older than you."

"It's so easy to forget that."

"Because I look so young?"

"Let's say that's the reason."

"That's odd," Said Honey. "The palace looks abandoned."

"How can you tell?" Asked Mathew.

"No one has gone in or out, and I haven't seen anyone through the windows. They wouldn't just, leave it would they? It's the perfect headquarters, somebody must have stayed."

"Then Ernloheim really is empty now." Said Alteem. He jumped off of the cart and started marching towards the palace.

"Where are you going?" Honey shouted after him.

"Alteem." Mathew and Alma called as they crawled out of the cart after him.

"Okay, I guess we're all leaving the cart now." The witch said steering the cart over and catching up with Alteem.

"See," She said. "We can just take the cart there, no big deal. I can even make it go faster." The cart rolled ahead of Alteem. "Just tell me where to go and we'll be there in no time."

Alteem ignored her as he continued his march towards the palace.

"Fine then," The witch said pouting.

The cart trundled alongside Alteem, the witch sliding into a reclined position.

Alma and Mathew followed behind. The Palace grew larger as they approached, until it blotted out most of the sky. The ruins of the outer city of Ernloheim lay about them, loose stones scattered everywhere. Alteem started to gather them and pile them up.

"I can help," said the witch.

"I don't want your help," said Alteem.

Alteem continued his work. After the first pile was nearly his own height, he created a trail of stones for several feet and started another pile. Over time he began to form a circle with his first pile at the center, a trail of stones connecting to all the other piles.

The former prince was halfway through his work when Honey sat up. "My old wardrobe." She said and ran towards the palace.

Alteem was nearly done with his work by the time she came out, sans wardrobe. "It was all looted," she said. "But they did have this." The witch held up a longsword, a crest depicting a Fjord on its pommel.

"My sword." Said Alteem. "My family's sword."

"I thought you might still want it. I had it locked away in my private vault." She held it out for Alteem to take.

His hand reached out for it, but stopped short. He stared at the sword, remembering. "I am not that person anymore." His hand dropped.

"Don't you still want it, it's all that remains of your family. Trust me, I know, I made sure of it."

"I have many memories of that sword. I remember seeing it on my father's belt. The day he gave it to me when I was officially made heir. A sword has purpose however, and the purpose is singular, that purpose is killing. I remember peasants who rebelled because their children were starving and there wasn't enough food to go around, or because they lived under a cruel lord. People called me a hero prince, but I still had all the same duties that other princes had. Let that sword rest with the dead."

Mathew took it from the witch and placed it upon the central pile of stones.

Alteem looked around at his circle of stones. "We should get going, I've wasted enough time here as it is."

"Don't talk like that," Said Alma. "It might not be much, but your people deserved something. Honey, is it possible there might be something else in the palace that could be of use to us? What else was in your private vault?"

"Some instruments of torture, some instruments of sex, some combinations of both. Also an accordion, which is so weird, like, I remember keeping it, but I don't remember why. What was even weirded was there was a kid inside the palace, and I'm positive I made sure to kill all the children around here."

"There was child inside the palace? A human child?" Alteem said a sudden intensity taking him over.

"I didn't stop to confirm it's species, but it looked human."

"We have to find them, we have to."

"Ick, no, we are not taking one of those disgusting little creatures with us."

"Where were they?" Alteem pleaded, stepping closer to the witch.

"I said no."

"We are not leaving a child behind in that place."

"Fine, we'll vote on it. Who's for leaving the child behind?" The witch raised her hand. A couple of moments passed without anyone else doing anything. The witch lowered her hand. "Voting is dumb when I don't get my way."

"There's no telling how long it could take to find the child in that place," said Mathew.

"I'll just activate the crystal golems and they'll find her," Said the witch

"Crystal golems?"

"They were a security measure I installed in case I ever lost control of the palace. They're built into the walls and come to life when I cast the right spell."

"You did lose control of the palace, you were deposed."

"I wasn't in the mood for it."

"When you first came to us," Said Mathew. "You wanted Alteem to raise an army so you could punish those who deposed you, and you had the means to do so before you even left the palace."

"First off, not all the leaders of the factions resided in the palace. They were all on a come and go basis, preferring to leave representatives most of the time. Second, many people fled in secret before they decided to confront me, fearing what I might do. Thirdly, I didn't just want to kill them, I didn't want them to rule, and given all the peoples I had in my army and lines of succession across several cultures tracking them down would have taken forever. Imagine the headache that would be. I needed a government to replace them so there wouldn't be a power vacuum any of them could fill. Fourthly, I wasn't in the mood for it."

"Just activate the golems so we can help this kid out."

"One army of brainless monstrosities coming up." The witch cracked her knuckles.

"Wait," said Alteem. "The golems won't kill the child will they?"

"Good catch, Alty, I did not think of that. I'll just modify the spell a bit." Honey wiggled her fingers and the palace shuddered. Everyone but the witch was knocked to the floor. Around them the ground quaked with the palace. It only lasted a moment, and from the outside nothing had changed. Honey was looking at her nails. "It's been too long since I last trimmed these." she said.

"You can't trim them with magic?" asked Mathew.

"I don't have a spell for nail trimming...yet." Honey pulled out a small booklet out of nowhere and wrote something down before it disappeared.

"Seems like it would be easy to do."

"Not if you don't mind your nails looking like yours."

"What's wrong with my nails?" Asked Mathew.

"Look at my nails, now look at yours, mine again."

"Yours are purple and weirdly sharp."

"Peasant." Honey said rolling her eyes.

"Why are your nails so sharp?"

"Intimidation?" Honey shrugged. "I made the decision when I could laid anytime I wanted to. I regret it now."

"What does that have to do with anything?"

"Given the state of your nails I'd say it's a good thing you don't know what I'm talking about."

"What is wrong with my nails?"

A golem emerged from the walls of the palace. Its body a mass of crystal shards with no discernable form. Held aloft in three rings of crystals were three children which it placed on the ground in front of the party.

"There was only supposed to be one, so, put that one and that one back."

"No," said Alteem.

"Are you going to kill us?" one of the children whimpered.

Alma walked up to the children and knelt down. "We're not going to hurt you," she said. "What are you three doing here?"

"The other kids said we'd be too scared to go inside the palace. Everyone says it's haunted," said the little girl.

"Shut up, Emily," said one of the boys.

"What other children?" Asked Alma.

"At the orphanage," Emily said.

"An orphanage, here? Who would start an orphanage here?"

"Aunty Ulwazi says it's the one place we can be sure the witch isn't anymore."

"Well," said Honey. "The kids are all safe and sound. Good work mister golem, back into the walls you go. I'm sure these children can all make it back on their own now. Have to keep moving as Alteem always likes to remind us."

"You know this Ulwazi?" said Alma.

"Why would you think that I know Ulwazi? I don't know any Ulwazi, she's probably just some old woman with a kind heart who's wondering where her three little darlings have run off to. Off you go children, back home where a nice warm meal is probably waiting for you."

"You're a terrible liar," Said Mathew.

"I know, but I've never had to practice. I've always been so powerful I could say whatever I wanted and no one could do anything about it. Sure it sounds like a lot of fun, and it is, but it's crippled my social skills. I don't know if you could tell."

Alma placed a hand on Honey's shoulder. "Everyone can tell."

"Is it that obvious?"

Alma nodded. "We can take you back home children, if you'll show us the way."

"What's wrong with your horse?" Asked the other boy.

"It's not a horse," said Honey. "It's a magical vortex that's constantly pulling an equivalent force in all directions. All a person has to do is temporarily lesson the force in a certain direction and the cart starts to move in the opposite direction."

"Can I touch it?"

"I don't care, go ahead."

"No," said Alteem. "It's dangerous."

"Come now, all of you. We'll help you onto the cart." Said Alma.

"Not on the cart," said Honey. "They'll get their gross children-ness all over it."

"Pay her no mind," said Alma. "She just gets crabby sometimes when she hasn't napped properly."

"So do I," said Emily.

Alteem lifted the children onto the cart one by one, then helped Alma up. After he climbed onto the cart, Mathew hopped up. Honey stood nearby her arms crossed. "Are you going to drive the cart?" Alteem asked.

"Yes," the witch said. "I'm just going to pout for a bit if you don't mind." And so she pouted for a bit, though everyone minded. After she finished, she climbed into her driver's seat and turned towards her passengers. "Which way?"

"That way," said Emily.

Honey flicked her hand, and the cart began to move.

Chapter 19

The cart trundled along the road, when they saw trees in the distance.

"There's a forest there," said Alteem.

"Yeah," said Mathew. "So."

"There didn't used to be a forest there."

"The forest moves," said Emily.

The trees in the forest didn't sway in the wind, but their leaves still shook. The grass inside it was a darker shade of green than the grass outside, and all the trees were gnarled in several places. They looked like old women gathered around to watch, and it did feel like they were watching anyone who came close enough.

As the cart entered the forest it felt as if the trees crowded around them, though they never saw them move. The smell of fresh cut wood hung in the air. Even the children who called this place home looked nervous under its canopy. Only Honey seemed not to care as she lounged in her seat.

Things constantly moved on the edge of vision as strange noises creaked and groaned in the distance. Tendrils of light peaked through the ceiling only to disappear suddenly. There came no sounds of bird, or animals though they heard fluttering.

They entered a glade and the witch stiffened. Jumping out of the cart, it came to a stop as soon as her feet left it. She ran to the end of the clearing and stared at the trees that loomed above her.

Mathew jumped off after her. "What's wrong?" He asked as he came up beside her.

"I killed these witches," Honey said.

"These are trees."

"They are gravestones," said Honey. "Different covens have different traditions. When witches of this coven die their magic returns to this forest and a tree is born."

"These trees are witches?"

"No, they're gravestones, pay attention. They carry with them some of the witch they once were, but they are not them. They are judging me."

"Gravestones that judge their killers."

"Judge, and move, and think. Too slow for most to notice, but it's there."

"I see, so this forest is the most terrifying graveyard in existence."

"No actually, there's this one graveyard in another dimension where you can hear the last words of the dead whispered over and over again when you get close to the graves. Also, the graves just appear there, no one knows how or why. And it's only people who die in terrible ways. Trust me, you don't want to go there. I've been to all kinds of dimensions of terror, but I peed a little when I walked through there."

"Why would you walk through such a place?" Asked Alma

"It was a dare." Said Honey.

"Do you always do everything you're dared to do."

"Not anymore, obviously, I've grown up since then."

"Have you?" Said Mathew

Alteem walked up to the witch and stood next to her. "What do they want from you?"

"I owe them a debt of blood too deep to pay," said Honey.

"Will they harm us?" Asked Alteem

"No," said Honey. "They want to see the children home."

"Then what are you doing?"

"There's so much I want to say to them. That I was wrong, that I'm sorry, but I don't feel like I deserve to say it. Sorry doesn't do the dead much good, does it? It would only assuage my own conscience. I still feel like I should tell them something. What would you say to the innocents you killed, if you had the chance?"

Alteem lowered his head in thought, said nothing, and walked back to the cart.

Honey turned to the trees, walked up to one of them and placed her hand on it. "I failed, but I am trying. I will do better." She whispered. Then she turned and ran back to the cart.

Mathew looked to the trees, then followed.

The cart proceeded through the glade and exited out the other side. It was near early afternoon when they came to the center of the forest. Here there was only one tree, large enough to be a house, which it was. The base forming an uneven oval, stretching a few stories high, but only slightly taller than the rest of the trees. Weaving its way through it was a wooden pipe. Whether it was part of the tree or had been installed later could not be gleaned from observation alone. The sound of trickling water came through the pipe.

Several children ran about the clear area surrounding the tree. A woman emerged from the green door which served as the main entrance. She was tall with bright eyes. Her hair looked like the setting sun and her skin was darker than the trees. She scanned the group, her entire body tensing up when she spotted Honey.

"I see you have brought three disobedient children," she said.

The children kept their eyes downcast as they climbed down from the cart. They drug their feet over to the woman.

"Where were you?" The woman asked them.

"We went to the witch's palace," Emily said.

"I told you how dangerous that place is," her eyes looked towards

Honey for an instant. "You're fortunate these people found you. Run along now, I'll deal with you later."

The children scampered off and the new witch approached the party. They exited the cart and stood in front of the woman. She was taller than all of them, even Alteem. "I am Ulwazi." She said. Turning from the group, her eyes studied the vortex in front of the cart, then she looked to Honey.

"Your dressed differently than usual," she said. "I suppose you're the good witch Kaytee I've heard whispers about. To think for a moment I dared hope someone truly good had appeared, and it turned out to be you."

"I am good now, I've renounced evil." Honey said.

The woman laughed, "You stupid little fool. Is that how you think it all works? A person is not simply good or evil. Everyone is both, and at times neither. You don't just renounce it and become good. Things are not black and white, there is only the shades of grey in between."

"Well no one told me that."

"Take off that idiotic disguise."

"No, this is how I dress now."

"You cannot simply change your clothes and erase your sins."

"I know, but I can't go walking around as myself."

"Why not? People should know if a monster is walking among them. I never dreamed I would see you again. I wish I had the power to kill you, after everything you've done."

"Well you don't, so we'll just leave you to your gross children and be on our way."

Ulwazi turned to Alteem. "I am curious, why does the last prince of Ernloheim travel with the enemy of all things, the person who destroyed the world, and eradicated his people?"

"I am not the prince of anything anymore, just a teacher with one very difficult student."

Ulwazi laughed, "She's your student? I've never heard anything so ridiculous and I have lived almost as long as she. What are you teaching her?"

"To be good."

"And is she learning."

"She can never make up for all that she has done, but better I teach her than she return to who she was."

"I suppose there is truth to that, but she does not deserve even a small amount of redemption." Ulwazi turned to Alma. "You I do not know."

"I'm her apprentice. My name is Alma." said Alma.

Ulwazi looked over at Honey, then back to Alma. "You're too old to be a witch's apprentice."

"She says she wants to try anyway and I'm willing to learn."

"Why do you want to learn magic, and from her of all people?"

"To help others if I can. There's a lot of good magic can do for poor peasant folk like me."

"There was once a coven of witch's who thought like you. Long ago, and the people they sought to help turned on them, and killed nearly all of them."

"Why would they do such a thing?" Alma frowned.

"Because they fear us, because we are different. Be wary where your quest leads you."

Ulwazi finally approached Mathew. "What are you, her lover?"

"Gross, no," said Mathew. "We're trying to stop the world from descending into war. Honey is the only one strong enough to ensure a peaceful transition. First we're going to find Sergei in the hopes he'll have some idea for how to organize new governments."

"Fitting the one who broke the world should try and fix it, but no matter what dress up she plays, she will never be anything but a monster. She cannot help you."

"As much as I hate her, you're wrong."

"What makes you believe in her?"

"Because she's amazing." Mathewsaid. "She's smarter and more capable than any person I've ever met. In the span off a few years she managed to organize universities across the world, and build roads. I watched her grow an entire forest in a few seconds, after having just learned the magic a few days earlier. She's the most exceptional person to have ever lived. If she conquered the world, then she can do anything."

"I don't deny her abilities. It's her nature that's the problem. Follow me, there is something you should see Alteem."

Ulwazi turned and started to walk away. Alteem glanced at his companions and then followed her. The others were not far behind him. They moved around the house to see a young woman playing with several children. Her hair was fair, her skin pale, and she had eyes of blue ice. She smiled at the children, but seemed sad.

There was only one person left alive who could have instantly placed the land her features came from, and he fell trembling to his knees before her.

The woman was startled by the behavior, and looked to Ulwazi. Ulwazi placed a reassuring hand on her shoulder. "The witch believed she managed to kill all the people of Ernloheim, save their prince. But when only smoke and ash remained I walked these lands. Normally walking so close would not have been safe, but the witch's attention and power was too focused on building her new palace to notice me. I did not believe I would find anything, but I was wrong. A babe cried out to me, cradled in a black cocoon that had once been her mother."

"Lauria," said Ulwazi. "This is your prince."

"I am no one's prince anymore," said Alteem. "But I am so sorry that when I was your prince. I failed you."

"You're Alteem," said Lauria. "I've heard stories of your heroism."

"And this," said Ulwazi. "Is Honeydrops, the witch that destroyed the world."

Honey gave a shy wave. "Nice to meet you."

Lauria's face twisted into fury and sorrow and she turned on Alteem. "Why are you traveling with her?"

"She has renounced her evil ways," said Alteem. "And now seeks redemption for her actions."

"She doesn't deserve redemption."

"It's rude to talk about someone when they're standing right there," said Honey. "Yet since we got here everyone keeps doing it."

"Do not speak to me again." Said Lauria.

"I think perhaps," said Ulwazi. "We should introduce Kaytee, the good witch, to the other children."

"What? Why?" said Honey.

Lauria looked confused, but bowed her head to Ulwazi. The girl started gathering up all the children. They all sat in a circle with the sun getting low.

Ulwazi waved her hand and a green fire appeared in the center of them. "Children," she said. "This is Kaytee, the good witch."

"You said all the good witches were dead." Piped up one of the older children.

"I thought they were," said Ulwazi. "Do any of you have any questions for Kaytee."

"How come the good witches didn't stop the bad witch?"

Honey suddenly grew stiff, her eyes locking onto Ulwazi for a moment. "They...we tried," she said to the children. "The witch, the bad witch, she anticipated the attack." Honey's face grew sad, and her eyes began to see things as she remembered. "It's common for witches, when they're still in training, to visit all the other covens. The bad witch never had any friends, aside from demons and monsters, but the women she met in the other covens were the closest she'd ever come. She liked them, but even then she was cunning and clever, and she had her plan."

Honey's hands began to shake as she spoke. "During her visits she gathered all the things from them she'd need to defeat them all. Pieces of hair, objects of their affection, articles of clothing, with these she had complete power over the other witches. When the covens united to try and stop her, their magic was useless against her. She killed most of them, all but one from each coven, so that the coven's might continue, but would never pose a threat to her again."

"Why would she kill people she liked?" Asked another child. "Why did she do all the bad things she did?"

"I don't know, she just, she thought if she could have everything, if she could rule the world, she'd be happy. If she made everything the way she wanted it, then she'd never feel bad ever again.

"Did it make her happy?"

"At first, sort of, her final victory was the first time she knew something like happiness. It was her moment. Everything was going to be better from then on. She reveled in all that she had done. An impossible feat that all who'd tried before her had failed."

"Didn't she feel bad for all the things she'd done?"

"She didn't think that other people mattered at all" Honey said, lowering her head. "It's what she'd been told her whole life."

"Do you think that people matter?"

"Yes, even the smallest of lives matter, because someone is living them."

"I think," Said Ulwazi. "It's time for a different story. One of a coven of good witches who existed in a time before people put words to symbols. witches were young then too, like all people, and not nearly as strong as they now are. That is when this coven formed, the first, and only, to ever dedicate themselves to do good and no evil. They wandered the world, helping crops grow, healing people, and bringing forth rains. So good were their deeds, it was said they made the moon smile. However, it is in the nature of humanity to distrust that which is different. For all the good they did, when a day came that they were not strong enough to heal a powerful plague, people accused them of causing it. Most were hunted down and killed. One witch survived, and in her anger she vowed vengeance. Whatever it took, her line would grow stronger with each generation, until one day, they would be strong enough to destroy all who had wronged them."

"You pick some weird storied to tell your kids," said Mathew.

"That's enough children," said Ulwazi. "Clean up time." She clapped her hands and the children began to clean up the large yard, picking up scattered toys and cleaning up messes."

"Can't you just use your magic to clean up after them?" Asked Alma.

"They must learn to take care of themselves. Eventually, they must all leave this place.

Even Lauria is older than I would allow most to stay, but she is a special case. Most I will drop off at a village as soon as they are old enough to make a living for themselves."

"You don't seem to have much compassion for them, even though you've taken them in."

"We are preservers in my coven. Mostly we preserve knowledge, like stories forgotten by everyone but us. Even if those whom the stories are about have forgotten it themselves. Sometimes we preserve plants or animals if we think it worthwhile, and in times of great need, we will preserve people."

"And what about the ones with skin like yours. Do they all have the same father, or have you used them to preserve different people as well?" Asked Honey.

"You noticed them, did you?" Said Ulwazi. "Of course I've had to start rebuilding my coven. I treat them the same as the other children when the others are around. I don't wish to build resentment towards them, there's enough resentment towards witches these days. I selected different father's for greater diversity. Always must we try and preserve."

"Yeah, yeah," said Honey. "I should say, even though I don't want to because I never liked you, but I have to say it because it's true. I'm sorry I killed your entire coven and your family."

"Why did you do it? We were no threat to you, always have we remained neutral."

"One thing I've learned, traveling across the world I destroyed, is that in order to be good, you must also believe in the goodness of others. The opposite is also true. When I was evil, I did not think people with power could avoid using it. I did not know what hidden knowledge your coven might use against me, so I struck before you could."

"You really are sorry aren't you?" Asked Ulwazi.

"Yes," said Honey. "I know I can't ever make up for what I've done, but I will spend the rest of my existence trying."

"I would have never thought to see it. What do you think Lauria?"

Lauria had snuck up behind Honey. There was suddenly a dagger in her hand, whose handle was shaped exactly like it's blade, and just as sharp. She grabbed Honey by her hair, and held the dagger to the witch's throat.

Blood dripped from Lauria's hand as she gripped the dagger tight. The blade touched Honey's neck, and a small trickle of blood appeared. "Look," said Lauria. "You bleed. I can cut you. I can kill you."

"Ulwazi," said Honey. "You didn't."

"I gave her a choice," said Ulwazi. "It is more than you ever gave her."

"I'm the one you have to pay attention to," Said Lauria. "Give me one reason I shouldn't kill you now."

"Do you truly wish to die?" Asked Honey.

"They will sing songs of my deed. I will walk the halls of my ancestors and join the eternal feast."

"You are so certain of what waits for you on the other side. I have been to many places people called hell, and some people called heaven. I met none of the dead there. Perhaps you should kill me, if anyone deserves to die it's me. You shouldn't die though. The dead are not honored with more death." Honey's hand moved faster than any eye could follow. She grabbed Lauria's wrist.

The girl struggled her whole body trying to move her hand, but the witch's grip was like steel, a purple mist floating around her.

"Let me go," said Lauria. "I will kill you."

The witch pulled the girl's hand away and twisted it. The dagger dropped to the ground, and Honey kicked it over to Ulwazi. "If you want me dead, sacrifice your own life instead of sending the children of other's to die in your stead."

"As I said," said Ulwazi. "I gave her a choice, it was what she wanted." Ulwazi stomped on the dagger and it shattered into glinting dust.

Honey let go of the girl's hand and Lauria fell to the ground, breaking into sobbing tears. Kneeling down beside her Honey, patted her on the shoulder. "There, there." She said.

"You have robbed me of everything," said Lauria. "I lived only because I thought I might kill you, what now shall I do without hatred to sustain me."

"Interpretive dance maybe?"

Lauria stopped her crying and turned to look at the witch. "What?"

"It worked last time," Said Honey. "But I guess it's not for everyone. There's lots of things to live for, there's flowers, cake, um, sex, have you had sex yet, it's pretty awesome. Well sometimes. Mathew come over here."

"No," said Mathew. "I'm not having sex with her."

"Not even to cheer her up? That's pretty uncool dude. Alma and Alteem are in a monogamous relationship. I'd do it, but I killed her whole family so that makes things pretty awkward. Ulwazi here is like, the closest thing she has to mother. Everyone else is a child. Come on, be a pal, she's above average looks wise."

"I don't want my first time to be with a man I don't know," said Lauria. "Plus it's a sin to do it without marriage."

"Bleck, what have you been teaching her Ulwazi?"

"Only the customs of her people," said Ulwazi.

"Fine then," said Honey. "I tried. Have some cake and ice cream, it's the next best thing." She snapped her fingers and a large chocolate cake appeared with a bowl of ice cream.

"What's ice cream?" asked Lauria.

"It's like a hug in food form. Okay, we're leaving." Honey said, walking up to Ulwazi. Honey might have been much shorter than the woman, but it was clear who held the power between the two of them. "I might be good now, but if you make another of those daggers I may have a lapse in judgement."

Ulwazi smiled, and Honey walked away. The witch got on her cart and motioned for the rest of the party to do so.

Chapter 20

The group was out of the forest, and back on the road. They'd continued on their journey deep into the night, not wanting to set up camp near the forest.

"What was that dagger?" Asked Alteem.

"It's had a few names over the millennia," answered Honey. "The simplest is the two bladed dagger. It can kill anything, bypassing all magical protections of any creature. But if it is used to take a life, it also takes the life of the wielder."

"That girl was going to take her own life in order to kill you?" said Alma.

"I would have done as much if given the option not long ago." Said Alteem.

"What does 'dude' mean?" asked Mathew.

"It's, just like saying, 'guy'." Said Honey.

"Oh, what language is it from?"

"Don't worry about it. It's from 9.34 dimensions away from here. She was crying, I didn't know what to do. I panic in situations like that. Next time someone cries I say we put Alma in charge."

"You just need to get better at comforting people," said Alma. "It helps if you can put yourself in their position. How would you feel if someone killed your family?"

"I killed my family," said Honey. "It was only my mother."

"What about your father?"

"My coven has always taken a praying mantis style of procreation, sans cannibalism."

"I don't know what that means," said Alteem. "But I'm glad it's sans cannibalism."

"The females kill and eat their mates, sometimes, some species do. My mother killed my father, my grandma killed my grandpa. There's a huge amount of killing each other in my family. Didn't make us a happy family," said Honey. "But I did conquer the world. Crimes against humanity aside, that's a great accomplishment. I do plan on breaking with the family tradition, of course."

"You might have conquered the world," Said Mathew. "But you didn't do a great job of ruling it."

"Conquering and ruling are different skill sets. I couldn't kill people into doing what I wanted. That's a problem all over the world, isn't it? Gaining rulership and being a ruler require different abilities."

"You didn't do so bad at the end," said Alma.

"I was just listening to the needs of the people so they'd shut up, and they still wouldn't shut up."

"That's what being a leader is," said Alteem. "We'll be coming to the mountain pass soon, that's where we leave Ernloheim."

"I started my conquest in these mountains, where the beastmen live. Took me forever to pick the right outfit, and then my hair, I almost put the whole thing off. It's important having the right look for things. Everyone tries to say, 'don't judge people by their looks' but everyone does it. Not the blind I suppose. They probably go by the sound of voices. Sometimes you'll hear the sound of someone's voice and you'll think, ooo, they sound sexy, then you see and them and it's nothing like you pictured. I'm not even saying they'll turn out ugly, just completely different than what you were thinking. Not even the right hair color."

"It must have been really hard for you when people wouldn't shut up," said Mathew.

"Don't even get me started," said Honey.

"How do I get you stop?"

Honey glared at Mathew, then snapper her fingers. Mathew yelped in pain.

"Mom, she's using magic against me."

"Honey, what have I told you about using magic against Mathew."

"I'm sorry Alma," said Honey.

They entered into the pass, it's once well-traveled roads now empty. It's loneliness bearing down from the high mountains on either side.

"Why was your family so concerned with conquering the word?" Asked Alma.

"Oh, who remembers?" said Honey. "You'd have to ask Ulwazi, they were the ones concerned with history. I just thought it would make me happy. I wanted everyone to have to do my bidding. Instead, you have to try and make everyone else happy. You end up doing their bidding. The whole thing is backwards."

Alteem laughed, "I remember how it all started. I was just sitting in my cell, suffering, hating you. Then you walked in, sat down, tears in your eyes. You looked around, the small purple light in your hand illuminating your face. Then you spoke, 'No one remembered my birthday' you said. I thought I'd finally gone mad. Maybe I did."

"I was so unhappy." Said Honey. "I've always been unhappy, and lonely. I sometimes wonder if I would even recognize happiness if I felt it. If the few times I thought I was happy I was just fooling myself."

"When were you happy?" Asked Alma.

"Like I said earlier, when I'd finally conquered the world. I was elated. Then the feeling passed, I came crashing down so hard and I felt so lost. I didn't know what to do, I had no one to turn to, I'd never felt worse in my whole life. The thing I'd bet everything on, the thing I'd torn the world apart to achieve, failed me. It hadn't changed anything. If that hadn't made me happy, then how could anything ever? I had trapped myself, and thought that because I had done it to myself I had to live with my choices. Then I turned out to be wrong again. Everything changed. I don't know if I can call myself happy now, or if I ever will be able to. I think, if I just keep walking down this path, I could be okay. That would be enough. Listen to me talk about this, after all I've done, I'm a monster."

No one said anything. They traveled through the rest of the valley in silence. On the other side the open plains stretched to every horizon. The only immediate sign of civilization was the ruined fort, blasted in half by the witch long ago. It had once stood as a defense for when the beastmen grew brave and risked coming out of the mountains. Now empty, it had only skeletons buried under rubble to keep it company.

"This was the first place you ever destroyed." Said Alteem.

"First human place, yes, but I had to subdue the beastmen first and I destroyed many of their villages." Said Honey.

"I'd hardly say that counts."

"What's that supposed to mean?"

"Your invasion started with this fort, the beastmen were just a stepping stone to that."

"The beastmen were the first people I conquered."

"They're not people."

"First demons, then goatmen, now the beastmen, you have a real problem Alteem. I suppose the Nestlings aren't people either."

"They're insects."

"Wow, okay, wow." Honey said. "Ulwazi was right, there are shades of grey, and you are SO grey right now."

"A person can't be more or less grey," Said Alteem. "Just darker or lighter shades. And you're barely even a shade lighter than pure black."

"Thank you." Said Honey.

"What? No, black is the bad color."

"Why is black the bad color?"

"Why wouldn't it be?" Asked Alteem.

"I like black." Said Honey.

"Black is bad, because people have a natural fear of the dark. The night, darkness, is black, and the day is white."

"No they're not, the night is more of a deep blue if you really look at the sky and the sun is yellow so why isn't the day yellow? Why isn't it yellow and blue with shades of green? This whole color based morality system makes no sense."

"What are you talking about!? You're insane, you are an insane person." Said Alteem.

"I think," said Alma. "The day is really more blue, sure the sun is yellow, but there's more sky than sun."

"That's a good point," said Honey. "Problem is then you have light blue and deep blue with shades of blue in the middle."

"What about when it's cloudy, then the days are grey." Said Mathew.

"Darkness is black," said Alteem. "White is the opposite of black, therefore black bad and white good."

"I don't know Alty," Said Honey. "I think morality might just be too complicated to express in colors."

"What if we thought of morality as a rainbow?" said Mathew.

"It's not the gradients that are the problem." Said Honey. "Things can be all over the place. Good things can have unforeseen terrible consequences, and bad things can end up having good consequences. When you think about it, how the hell is anyone supposed to know what to do?"

"No one does," said Alteem. "Everyone just does the best they can."

"Do they?" Asked Honey.

"Yes," Said Alteem, pausing to think about it. "Yes they do."

"I've seen people, they frequently choose not to do the best they can. Look at me, I did way worse than the best I could."

"What about, everyone does the best they know how?"

"Still no."

"Everyone is trying as hard as they can." Said Alteem.

"Are they?" Asked Honey

"Mostly."

"Hmmm."

"Mostly mostly."

"Seems to me people just do whatever's most convenient at the time and then rationalize it as the right thing to do."

"People do do that." Said Alteem. "If you think so little of people then why are you trying to be good?"

"I just went over that, so I can be happy or as close as I can get to it. Why else would anyone try to be good?"

"Everyone *tries* to be good."

"They don't do a very good job. Again, prime example sitting right here."

"I don't know," said Alteem. "This was all a lot easier when you trusted I knew what I was talking about."

"I've been learning," said Honey. "And I learn quickly. You've got some problems with other species."

"I do not."

"You're a speciesist."

"I don't what that is, but I'm not it."

"You think humans are better than all the other species."

"I do not."

"Admit it, in your mind the whole world would be better if humans were the only ones around."

"It would certainly be more peaceful."

"I've been to those places and nope."

"Fine, maybe I do think humans are better than goatmen and beastmen and the nestlings, but it's only because we are."

"Speciesist."

"What does it matter?"

"It matters because we're trying to make peace."

"Yeah, for people."

"For everyone."

"You really think people are going to be okay with the goatmen, beastmen, and nestlings coming to the negotiating table after what they did, after they joined with you."

Honey raised her eyebrows at Alteem, who shrunk away from her gaze. "There can't be peace without them, and plenty of humans joined me."

"I don't recall any beastmen coming to the call of the last alliance."

"I do, you didn't trust them."

"How do you know that?"

"Spies, duh."

"How could I trust them, when they were all in your employ."

"No they weren't. How could you trust humans when they were also in my employ? And, as it turns out, you couldn't, because some of them were my spies."

"Would one of you two back me up on this?" Alteem asked, turning to Mathew and Alma.

Mathew shrugged, "Some of the beastmen went to University with me. They were just like anyone else. Only problem was they're not a gender dimorphic species so you couldn't ever tell if they were male or female. Seemed rude to ask so you had to use a lot of neutral pronouns."

"Fine," said Alteem. "I'm just wrong about everything."

"Not everything," said Honey. "But this. Why do think the nestlings joined me? They had no fondness for me. The only reason they took slaves was because everyone else did. They never even used them for work, since they actually enjoy manual labor. Their slaves just sat around and did whatever. The nestlings weren't violent, but I offered them a peaceful existence, humanity only ever offered them war. People will make a deal with the devil if they're not allowed into heaven."

"They're insects, not people."

"Wow, just, wow."

Chapter 21

The party was approaching another town when they noticed people screaming and running away.

"I'm starting to think we have a moral responsibility to avoid towns," said Honey.

"We're not causing these things to happen," said Alteem.

"Starting to seem like we are."

"That's ridiculous."

"Everywhere we go this happens."

"Doesn't mean we're causing it. But it does mean we can do something about it."

"Yeah, fine."

The cart spurred forward into the town. A group of armed men were ransacking the town. They didn't directly attack anyone unless they tried to stop them, but they were loading all the food they could find into carts. At the center, shouting orders was a man with black hair and red eyes.

He turned to look at the cart as it came into view, his eyes meeting the witches.

"Flamelash," she said.

"Honeydrops," he said.

"How are you? I haven't seen you in forever."

Flamelash's eyes darted to Alteem, then back to Honey. "What are you doing here?"

"I turned good, got a new persona, Kaytee."

"Of course *you're* Kaytee, and here I'd hoped for something good in the world. What are you going to do now that you're here?"

"I'm a good guy now, well, a good woman. Saying good woman has an entirely different implication doesn't it? Good girl? No, that's worse."

"Focus, please." Said Flamelash, almost automatically.

"Right sorry, I'm good and you're bad. I wish I could give you a pass for old time's sake, but you know how it is."

"Of course," said Flamelash. "Everyone retreat!"

The men looked at Flamelash confused.

"Now!" He found a horse and jumped onto it, spurring the beast away.

"You know," said Honey. "Sometimes if you haven't seen a person in a while you forget their negative traits. I forgot how rude he could be."

"Shouldn't we go after him?" said Alteem.

"Yeah, fine," said the witch. "I was excited to see him. You'd think he could have shown a little courtesy." Standing on the cart, she raised up one of her hands and purple tendrils emerged from the wood. They wrapped themselves around the party and the plant, securing them to the cart. More tendrils emerged in front of the witch, and she grabbed them in her hands like reigns. The cart rocketed forward, causing everyone in the back to lurch, but the tendrils held them in place.

Blasting through the village, it did not take long for them to catch up to Flamelash who was galloping his horse as fast as it would go.

He turned to glance at the witch without slowing, "What do you want?"

"First off, I'd like an apology for that rudeness back there." She said, bringing her cart up beside him.

"You know how if you haven't seen a person in a while you start to forget some of their negative traits."

"Yes I do, we were just talking about that."

"I forgot how annoying you are."

"Oh."

"I remembered that you were annoying," said Flamelash. "Just not the extreme degree."

"Now I think I'd like two apologies." Said Honey.

"You'll get none and you deserve none."

"And here of all my underlings you were my favorite."

"And you were an evil hell bitch who destroyed the world."

"You helped."

"I only did what I have always done," Said Flamelash. "Tried to find a place in the world for those who have none."

"That justifies stealing from people who have done you no wrong."

"Justifies, perhaps not, but it does necessitate it."

"Can you two maybe stop and then have this conversation?" Mathew yelled from the back.

Flamelash glanced back, then pulled his horse to heel. The cart pulled ahead, but came to a stop and wheeled around. The bandit moved his horse up to the back of the cart. "You, Alteem, last prince of Ernloheim, how have you found yourself keeping such company."

"It's not as if there's a way to make her go away." Said Alteem.

Flamelash let out pronounced laugh. "I don't remember you being funny."

"The last time you saw me I was being hauled away in chains after failing the world, wasn't in the mood for jokes."

"And here you are, with your greatest enemy."

"Enough Flamelash," said Honey. "I can't let you perform banditry anymore."

"Will you kill me then?" Asked Flamelash

"I'm not here to kill you, but you have to stop now."

"I cannot stop, if I do, people will starve."

"And what of those you would steal from, will they not starve. If there's anything now, it's space. You can make a home for your people anywhere you wish."

"And who will teach us to live? I am not a farmer. We are criminals, cast out by everyone from everywhere. Exiles, outcasts, sick, lame, half breeds, deformed, soldiers plucked from poor families, used up, and cast aside when there were no more wars to fight. There is no other way to live for us."

"I didn't cast you out."

"No, but you did leave. Do you think there was a place for us among your hordes the moment you vanished? They did not wait to turn on each other, and we were the first they turned on. Maybe now there's more war brewing some can turn back to mercenary work. Until those wars end too and they have to come back again."

"I will stop the wars."

Flamelash laughed again. "You don't stop wars, you cause them. The truth is you didn't cast us out because you're one of us. The only difference is you have power, and we are powerless. The only things anyone ever gets in life is what they take, you're able to take more than most."

"That doesn't make any sense."

"Why not?"

"Can't something be earned instead of taken? Like, if a farmer grows something haven't they earned it through their hard work?"

"They...take it from the earth."

"Oh come on, that's pretty weak. What about bakers baking bread, or prostitutes?"

"They say prostitution is the oldest profession."

"Couldn't possibly be."

"Why not?"

"Because it's the exchange of currency, goods, or services for sex. Necessarily, a person would have to have one of the things in order to exchange it, and would therefore have to have a profession predating prostitution."

"I see your point. Do animals have professions? What's a squirrel's profession?"

"Gatherer I'd think." Said Honey.

"I suppose all animals are hunter/gatherers." Said Flamelash.

"Not dogs, we train them to do other things."

"That's true."

"And some elephants."

"Horses."

"You're sitting on one now."

Flamelash patted his horse. "There's also farm animals."

"What about them?" Asked Honey.

"Their job is to be food."

"A whole existence spent eating only to be eaten. That's depressing to think about."

"Yeah."

They paused, thinking about the implications of such a thing.

"So about stopping the banditry?" Honey said, breaking the silence.

"As I said, can't do it."

"And I can't let you continue, seems we are at an impasse."

"You were never one to tolerate an impasse."

"What if," said Alma. "We found someone to teach you how to start a new life. Make a land of your own. Till the soil and give farm animals depressing lives. To teach your people trades and other skills you'd need."

"Some would not wish to change." Said Flamelash.

"Then they have no excuse for what they do and no reason to complain about what happens to them." Said Honey.

"Alright, I'll agree to give you a chance to find someone, or given the scale of things find several someone's to teach us. But, if you fail, and you will, then you will leave us and be on your way."

"Perfect, I know just the person. I'll just need a baby to sacrifice."

"No baby sacrifices," said Alteem.

"Sorry, I forgot. That does make things a little harder. What about, a basket of puppies."

"Also no."

"Come on, they're just puppies. Too many strays in the world as it is."

"I said no."

"Kittens?"

"No baby anything."

"The first born calf of a first born calf, it can be full grown."

"What happens to it?"

"Let's skip the gorier details. It ends with total incineration."

"Is there any way to do what you need to do without sacrificing anything living?"

The witch paused to think. "How attached are you to the moon?"

"Let's find a calf."

"We might have one at our hideout." Said Flamelash.

"Cool, a hideout," said Honey. "Is it like a bunch of connected tree forts?"

"No, why would anyone build anything so complicated for a hide-out."

"It would be cool."

"It would be so easy to just chop down some trees, or light them on fire. You'd have no good way of defending yourself."

"I'd forgotten how concerned you always were with the practicality of things."

"Not all of us have godlike power."

"That's what you always say."

"No one ever always-"

"No one ever always or nevers! I know! I remember the counseling you all made me go through."

"You didn't remember it enough to not accuse me."

"What happened?" Asked Alteem.

"This was after you left." Said Honey. "I had no one to talk to I started to get little cranky."

"She kept threatening to blow up the planet." Said Flamelash.

"Can you?" Asked Alteem.

"You never know what you're capable of until you try." Said Honey.

"Don't try."

"I won't...as long as there's still people on it."

"We should get going to the hideout if we're going to do this." Said Flamelash

"The thing people don't know is that the center of the planet is a molten core, so if you could somehow cause that to expand rapidly then, BOOM! Goodbye planet." Said Honey.

"Why have you thought it out that far?" Asked Alteem.

"Wouldn't you want to know if you could?"

"No, I wouldn't even consider it."

"I'll just go on ahead, you guys can catch up." Flamelash started moving his horse again.

"Think about it, if you can blow up a planet, then maybe you could blow up a star." Said Honey.

"Why would you want to blow up a star!?" Asked Alteem.

"TO SEE IF I COULD!!! Don't you listen?"

Chapter 22

After working their way through the list of things Honey wanted to blow up (just to see if she could), the party followed Flame-lash to his hideout. The place was a makeshift, half village and half fortress. A wooden palisade snaked through buildings. Huge gaps appeared in it where it had been torn down and was in the process of being rebuilt around new structures. Things towards the center looked more permanent, having been constructed first and reinforced over time with greater conviction. Near the edges was mostly tents, and sometimes not even that. Sleeping spots with blankets and a fire was all that decorated certain locations.

Everywhere was a mish mash of people. Some wore old metal armor, covered in dents and scratches with worn out standards of dead households. Others wore leather and chain with mercenary etchings upon them. Many people were sick with boils or rashes covering parts or sometimes all of their bodies. There were those missing limbs, or who sat sightless and hopeless, staring into nothing. Those with deformities were the most chipper of the lot. Smiling more than the others, they moved about taking care of those who couldn't care for themselves. A hunchback carried sacks of bread handing them out to the sick. One person covered in hair fed soup to the sick. A person who wore a cloth sack over their head read a story to a group of children all suffering the same sickness.

"Here they are," said Flamelash. "People welcome nowhere else are welcome here. Still believe you can make a normal world for them."

"First things first," said Honey. She hopped off the cart and placed a hand upon the earth. A purple miasma appeared around her hand and billowed outward towards the camp. The first who saw it attempted to run, but it spread so fast they didn't even have time to get to their feet before it enveloped them. The miasma covered all those it touched and all sickness was sucked out of them. Those missing limbs regrew them and those without sight or hearing regained them. The deformed were remade, and by the time the miasma was done not even a pimple remained in the camp.

It retracted in an instant, all sucked up into a small swirling ball of purple in the witches hand. She gingerly placed it on the cart. "I'll just put that there for now, nobody touch it please."

"When did you learn to that?" Asked Flamelash.

"I know," said Honey. "I'm even more impressive than the last time you saw me."

"I hate to contribute to your unhealthy attitude of extreme self-love and self-hate, but, yeah, you are."

"Ah thanks, you're too kind. And to answer your question, I learned the basics a long time ago, but I've been working on a way to do it without touching people since then and this was my first test run. Only problem is it leaves one of those behind." She pointed to the ball on the cart.

"When did you find time to practice that?" Asked Alteem.

"Sometimes I run off to work on new magic and leave you guys with an illusion of me."

"That explains the long periods of quiet," Alteem smiled to himself.

"Why were you smiling when you said that?"

"I wasn't smiling."

"Yes you were."

"I wasn't."

"I saw you, you were smiling."

"It's because you're annoying." Said Mathew. "And it was nice when you finally shut up."

"Oh." Said the witch. "You could've just said." Honey crossed her arms.

"I didn't want to hurt your feelings." Said Alteem.

"My feelings aren't hurt."

"Yes they are."

"Don't tell me if my feeling are hurt or not. You're not in charge of my feelings."

"I don't have to be in charge of them to know that they're hurt. You always act like you're okay but it's clear when you're not."

"I'm fine!"

Everyone around them winced.

"What?" Said the witch.

"Oh Honey," Said Alma. "Everyone knows 'I'm fine' is code for not fine."

"Yeah, everybody knows that." Said Flamelash. "Not the words themselves, but when they're said in that tone."

"I don't have a tone." Said Honey.

"You clearly had a tone," said one of the people from the camp.

"Who are you?"

"I'm Ted."

"Go away Ted!"

"Don't lash out at Ted," Said Flamelash. "He's a nice guy."

"It's okay Flamelash, I know it's not about me." Said Ted.

"Enough," said Honey. "Just bring me a calf so I can ritually slaughter it and summon a demon."

"Should you be ritually slaughtering when you're in this state?" Asked Alma.

"I'm fi-" Honey took a moment to glare at everyone. "Just get me the stupid calf."

"When you're ready to finally talk openly about your feelings, I'm here for you." Alma patted Honey on her shoulder.

"I miss the days when I'd just kill people who annoyed me." A brief flash of purple energy crackled in one of the witch's hands.

"That's not a healthy way to deal with your problems."

"You're my apprentice, go back to cosmos breath."

"I'll go get the calf." Said Flamelash. He moved deeper into the camp. When he returned, he was leading a calf by a leash, the creatures shoulders taller than the bandit's waist. "Will we...be getting the calf back?"

"It's a 'sacrifice'...unless we're willing to relax the no baby murder rule. This place *is* on the destitute side of things. There's bound to be an unwanted squirming around somewhere. We can fudge it a little if necessary. I'd be willing to accept a toddler."

Flamelash wordlessly handed over the leash for the calf.

"Okay," she said. "It's probably best if I do this out of sight. People are welcome to watch if they want, but only if it remains a judgement free zone."

"Just go do it." Said Mathew.

The witch led the calf away, till she was out of sight.

"So, Flamelash" said Alteem. "When you served her, did you know she was sacrificing babies?"

Flamelash turned and walked deeper into his camp.

The witch was gone for the rest of the day. It wasn't until the full moon hung in the sky that she returned, covered in blood. Only the upper left half of her face remained clean.

"Let me just say," the witch began. "Cows have so much more blood than babies. I was **not** ready for that."

"Is it done?" asked Alteem.

"Nearly," the witch held up a jar filled with black ash. "I'm gonna need everyone to eat this. Where's Flamelash? He has to eat it too since he's the one who needs help."

"What is it?" Asked Mathew.

"Cow ash," said Honey. "What else would it be?"

Flamelash appeared from out of the camp. "That took you much longer than I expected."

"A less valuable sacrifice requires more time. Anyway, eat this, all of you, come on."

Everyone took a handful of the ash. They each took different amount and examined it in their hands. Everyone took their time before finally eating it, but each took a different amount of time. When Alma finally gave in, the witch burst into laughter.

"We didn't need to eat that, did we?" Asked Mathew.

Still laughing Honey said. "I just wanted to see if you would. We should see who else we can get to eat it. Maybe that one guy with the sack on his head."

"No." said Flamelash. "You promised us help. Where is it?"

"You never were much fun," said Honey. She took a nearby stick and dipped it into the ash. Writing a circular ruin on the ground, she almost danced as she made it, whirling around with different strokes of the stick. After she finished, she tossed the stick aside and snapped her fingers.

The light around them tinged red and blood washed over the moon in the sky. A massive portal, thrice as tall as the nearby trees, appeared. Its outer edges were crimson, but it's center was a black vortex. When looked at the viewer could hear the distant cries of anguish. A figure stepped out of it, just as tall as the portal, when its goat-like hooves touched the ground the earth rumbled. People in the camp began to run and scream at the sight of it.

The creatures skin was flame and ash, the night lighting up around him. It had two arms such as a humanoid creature would have, but from its back sprung forth six more arms like wings. Each had four joints and their clawed hands held different jagged blades that burned with black flame. Its chest was an open cavity with exposed ribs that dripped with blood so dark it was close to black. When the blood fell to the ground it burst into flame before quickly burning out. Inside the rib cage several birdlike creatures perched on the bones and circled about in flight. They had human skin and faces, and their mouths were constantly open in wordless screams as streams of blood poured out of their eyes like tears. Sharp nail-like talons sprouted from their feet. The demon had no face, but the flames that burned their way across his body would take shapes that looked like eyes.

A voice emanated from the demon's body. It sounded dry and hoarse, like the last word of a man dying from thirst. "Who dares summon the great Bali'omerith'baenliish"

"Bob!" Said Honey. "Bob it's me."

The demon knelt down. "Honeydrops, is that you?"

"Hey, how you been?"

"Well, I live in a literal hell, but good otherwise."

"How are the kids?"

"As well as can be expected, She'erish got her first summon. I had to kill and eat Yob'norc'ali after he tried to overthrow me."

"I was never a fan of the harsh disciplinary methods, but I know you're doing your best."

"I think after he's digested over an eon he'll have learned his lesson. So, you want me to destroy this town?"

"No, actually, I need you to teach them agriculture."

The demon did not have facial expressions, so it was hard to read, but it seemed shocked. Then came laughter, and the creatures in its chest voiced their screams as the demon laughed before going silent again. "You really had me going there."

"I'm serious, I decided to turn good. They need help, and I remember how you told me your real passion was agricultural science."

"I told you that in confidence."

"Don't worry, everyone here is cool."

"The thing is, I'm not much of a teacher. I'm currently digesting one of my own children. That should give you some idea of how I handle things."

"I see your point. I wouldn't want you eating anybody. Perhaps you could learn together."

"Sorry, but I just can't see it working out."

"I went to all the trouble of summoning you, there must be something you can do?"

Bob stroked one of his exposed ribs, thinking, "There's a beastman I know who's learned agriculture and taught it to other beastman. I only know of him because he used to worship me, but stopped once he started farming."

"That's perfect. "Said the witch.

"No, it's not." Said Flamelash. "I'll not have some monsters mingling with my people."

"I did not see the mixed blood with you." Said Bob.

"Do not call me that, creature," Flamelash glared at Bob.

"How many of the humans think of you as a creature? Perhaps you only cling to your humanity so eagerly because it is not complete. That is why you look down on the beastmen. You do not wish to acknowledge you are like them."

"I am not like them. They are animals."

"You will accept them," said Honey. "Because it is the only chance for your people."

Flamelash glared at Honey with his red eyes, then stormed off into his camp.

"I shall go and bring the farmer." Said Bob.

Honey nodded, and Bob stepped back through the portal he came from. It disappeared as soon as he did so.

Chapter 23

The next day the camp was significantly smaller.

"Where did everyone go?" Honey asked Flamelash.

"Home," he said. "I should have realized it right away, but..." He broke off part of a stick he was holding and threw it. "After you healed them there was no reason they couldn't go back to the life they knew. Their deformities is the only reason they stayed here. The only reason they followed me. Once that was gone, they went back to the world that rejected them.

"Who's left?"

"Exiles, those whose wounds could not be healed the same way a missing limb can be."

"And you."

"And me. Others come and go, but I will never belong. There is a part of me that no people will ever accept."

"You're not alone in that. I've never belonged either. At least you didn't conquer the whole world to try and change that."

"I helped," Flamelash gave a weak smile. "What about Kaytee, the good witch. Does she belong?"

"No," said Honey. "She's not real, just a lie that stops people from running and screaming when they see me."

The portal opened up again, and through it stepped the demon once more. This time people did not run and scream in terror. It's amazing how quickly people can get used to something. Following him through the portal were several beastman, though they did not look the usual sort, or more accurately, they did not look how beastman usually looked. They had no armor, nor weapons, but wore peasant clothes, shirts and pants, and those without hooves wore shoes.

The one at their front had the ears of a wolf, the eyes of an owl, and the mouth of a human. "Uh, greetings." He said. He held a cane in one clawed hand, the other much more like a humans held a book. "We were told there were some lost souls in need of our aid. Not the usual thing a demon comes asking about, but we're here we are all the same." He was not dressed as the others but wore a robe with two red stripes coming from the shoulders down.

"Yes, hello," said Honey. "I'm Kaytee, the good witch."

"Oh, I thought all the good witches had perished."

"Just mostly," said Honey with a hand wave. "This is Flamelash, former bandit king, and future farmer."

"No," said Flamelash. "The purpose of your coming here has gone, beast. Go back to whatever slum you crawled out of."

The beastman bristled a bit at the comment but did not rise to anger. "There are still some here, do they not need aid. And my name is Tumon."

"They do not, beast."

"I think they should be asked themselves."

"Yes," said Honey. "Let's ask them."

It took time, to find every one left in the camp, but with some urging from Honey they got everyone gathered.

"Good, great, now everyone's here," Said Honey. "This is Tumon, and he has come to teach you all about agriculture."

"I can speak for myself," said Tumon.

"Oh, okay."

"I know the perceptions of my kind, but surely you all too have been judged unfairly by others who only looked at you." Tumon's head turned to Flamelash for a moment before addressing the crowd. "Just as all humans are not the same, neither are we. My people have sought a different path. It seems those of you who wished to build a new life for yourselves have gone, but I can see in your eyes wounds of the soul. So it was with me, once. I committed many a terrible acts of savagery.

"One day, in battle, after raiding a town my own clan turned against me for they coveted my loot. I lay dying, my blood leaving my body from several wounds. A man found me, I thought he meant to finish me. Instead he bandaged my wounds, and built a gurney for me. He took my body many miles, tending to me as needed to save my life. I drifted in and out of consciousness."

"When I awoke, I was weak, but able to walk again. I found myself attended to by several people in a room. I went to the nearest window to see where I was. When I opened it, I found myself in the same village I had raided when I was wounded. At first, I thought these people a fool to save an enemy. At the same time I wanted to know why they would do such a thing.

"During my recovery, I asked them many questions. Theirs was a way of life dedicated to peace and the preservation of all life. I laughed at them many times, but when I was recovered I found I did not want to leave. I stayed with them many years, learning their way of life. In that time I learned that while my physical wounds had healed long ago, I had other wounds that were still being healed. If violence wounds us, it can then only be peace that truly heals us. This was the ultimate lesson I learned from them.

"So I departed, to teach others of my kind their ways. Most would not listen, as I did not think they would, but some did. Soon I had many followers and I at last returned to the place that had saved my life and transformed it. I found it destroyed by the witch. I would never understand why, but me and my followers took up their place.

Anyone is welcome to join us in peace, so that their bodies and hearts may be healed."

"Anyone?" asked Honey, her eyes glistening with tears.

"Anyone." Said Tumon.

"Anyone?" asked Bob, his hand thoughtfully resting on one of his ribs.

Tumon laughed, "Anyone."

A few people walked over to stand with Tumon, but the rest remained near Flamelash, looking to him. Flamelash looked to his people, then at Tumon, then towards Honey, who tilted her head several times in Tumon's direction. He walked over, and stood with Tumon.

"And you, Bob?" Tumon asked.

"Another lifetime, perhaps," said Bob. "But I have obligations in hell. For now, it's best I see you back home."

"You must join us, Kaytee," said Tumon. "Today is a day to celebrate, with so many joining us."

"A celebration!" The witch said, hopping a few time with excitement and looking to Alteem.

"Where is this place?" Asked Alteem.

"A good deal further east of here," said Tumon.

"It would bring us closer to our destination," said Alteem. "We can spare one day to gain many."

"Yay!" the witch squealed clapping her hands.

"Come then," said Bob, leading them into the portal.

There are many places that claim to be THE hell, but really there are many such locales. As to where they came from, people have put forward a number of different hypothesis. Some think they were all imagined into being. Others have pointed out that people imagine all sorts of things that never come into being, so what the hell makes people think hell is so special?

Others simply believe that in the grand scheme of the cosmos with its endless universes, sometimes people are just going to end up with the shit end of the stick. Why people keep keeping shit on one of the ends of the stick, no one knows.

Another hypothesis is that none of these places started out so bad, but, people being people, fucked it up.

Some hells are blazing hot, a wild inferno that boils the flesh and each breath scorchers the lungs, others a cold so freezing is bites and stabs at the skin while freezing eyes open, one hell in particular is only chilly, but no one is allowed extra layers. This hell, as the Flame-lash's refugees would discover, was hot yes, but worse was the oppressive humidity. Anyone who's ever known such humidity can tell you, it's hell. Humidity has this way of sapping you of your will to live, which doesn't help if you're already dead.

A bit of warning about what to expect wouldn't have hurt as the people fwipped away through the portal. It is doubtful, however, that much could be done to ever prepare a person for a trip through hell.

After getting as accustomed as people can get to the constant sticky feeling that goes with heavy humidity, people took a look around. Nearby demons were pealing the skin of a group of humans using only their finger nails.

"Oh," said the witch. "That's where I had my first kiss. His name was Alzsaphar. He had two mouths and three tongues. The third tongue was just above his penis."

"Right," said Bob. "Nobody wander off lest you get lost or lose your soul. Let's be quick about it, no one wants to stay longer than they have to."

Everyone huddled close together, despite the climate, and stepped quickly through hell.

"Right over there," said Honey, pointing to a field of demonic bodies and limbs. Some were cut, but others had teeth and claw mark upon them. Maggots and flies swarmed the field so heavy it was a dark cloud over a squirming sea of white. "A great battle happened there.

I was so young then. Very few times have I been able to unleash my fullest power, but on that day I rent hell asunder. It twas glorious, though they did make me fix it."

"Ah yes," Said Bob. "Some of those nega-demons came through the rift. Stopped the war just to fight them off."

"What's a nega-demon?" Asked Mathew.

"They're like demons but more, nega."

"Nega-demons." Said Honey. "Are to demons what demons are to humans. Not exactly, but that's the best way to explain it. In fact, I'd say it goes humans, demons, nega-demons, abominations, void drifters, void shifters, sentient jalapenos, and finally, of course, the others."

"Don't talk about them." Said Bob.

"What are the others like," asked Mathew.

"They're not so bad," Said Honey. "They just consume reality where ever they show up."

"That sounds bad."

"What's so great about reality?" Honey shrugged. "Plus they mostly just consume the past, it's not like anyone's using it anymore anyway. Gotta say, hell doesn't seem to be affecting you that much, Mathew."

"It's not as bad as the Dimension of Agony."

"True, hell is hell, but the Demonsion of Agony is literally made up of agony in the way our universe it made up of atoms. We breathe air, they breathe agony, we get heat from the sun, they get agony from the agony, we eat food, they eat a breed of flower that only grows there and is supposedly more delicious than anything in our dimension, but it comes with a side of agony."

They walked past a pool of boiling diarrhea that people were being dipped into. "I used to play there when I was a kid." Said Honey. "So many memories here."

The journey through hell eventually came to an end and emerged into a city of green and golden brown. It existed at the end of a valley, with mountains on one side and tall hills on the other. The city was built upon many different levels, with each one being a flat area of grass with three or four square houses made of the golden brown bricks. Stairs divided each section, though in some cases the divide was so small it wasn't necessary. The whole thing was an uneven patchwork going up and down at random. On top of the houses was more green, as dirt had been piled on top of them for gardens. Streams and small waterfalls flowed everywhere, sometimes the streams even flowing over the houses that were built into the walls of particularly large divides.

Towards the mountains could be seen even more waterfalls, much bigger, pouring out of the mountains. The hills held the farmlands, organized not in divides but in rolling lands where people plowed the fields with oxen.

"Welcome," said Tumon. "To Therene, city of peace."

"Oh," Honey whispered to Alteem. "I remember this place now."

"As with most places these days," said Tumon. "There's plenty of space, so finding homes for everyone should be easy. First, I shall show those planning on staying around. The rest of your will find a fine place to rest at our first destination."

The first place he took them was a building that had a divide all to itself. It stood three times as tall as the others with stone columns propping it up. "This is where our scholars work, doing their best to study medicine and engineering in the hopes of making life better for everyone. There are many benches and murals along the walls as well as books and scrolls to study. Those of you who do not wish to live here may make your leisure time here while I help the others get acquainted, and of course, prepare the celebration."

Tumon left the original party alone while the others followed him.

"Finally," said the witch. "A real celebration."

"Why did you do it?" Asked Mathew.

"Do what?"

"Kill the people who used to live here."

"They were there," said Honey with a shrug.

"They didn't try to resist you in any way."

"Neither did they submit to me."

"So you killed them."

"I was wrong, I know, I'm just answering your questions."

"I keep thinking I'll get used to how much misery you caused the world, but it always gets worse."

"You were really young when I first conquered the world, so let me paint a picture. Imagine way more people than there are now, like, four times as much. Those extra people, I killed them all, I killed most of the people. Not all directly, but a great deal I did. So many I can't count, four digits, definitely, five, maybe. I have tortured, I have maimed, I have laid waste to armies and cities with a wave of my hand. I poisoned most of the surface of planet with foul magic so that nothing could grow, and that is how most people died. From hunger and starvation, friends turning upon friends, sometimes families devouring each other, at times literally. And that was exactly how I planned it."

"But why?"

"I have said many times now, because I thought it would make me happy." Honey turned away from the rest of them. She leaned against one the pillars and hugged her arms around herself.

"You talk of other worlds, why not conquer one of them?" Asked Mathew.

"I know you're not familiar with the rules interdimensionality, but it's considered very rude to conquer a world other than your own. People come after you. Yes, there's stories of demons trying to conquer other worlds, but those are just stories. Demons like to come in and wreck a little havoc, but only when invited. Elder gods on the other hand, don't even get me started on those self-important assholes. 'Look at me, all other beings are meaningless because I exist' what a load of shit. They're always going on about how they're going to conquer other worlds and they don't care about the rules, but do they, no. If they do everyone would kick their sorry asses back to their own weird little universes where they can't even get architecture right.

"You want to talk scary, let's talk about the dimensions where the 'good gods' rule. They call it heaven, but all it is, is a bunch of weird socially awkward people with blank expressions of mindless contentment bowing over and over again to whatever entity they call their god and singing its praises."

"How did you get into any place called heaven anyway, and why?" Asked Alma.

"They don't really guard them well, everyone's too busy worshipping their narcissistic 'gods' to enjoy the paradise around them. They have the best beaches, and no one is using them. No sharks, no sunburn, no trash, just the endless white sand and the perfect shade of bluegreen for the water."

"Sounds nice."

"Yeah, but the food isn't as great as you think. Everything has to be 'good for you' and not even heaven can make that stuff palatable. I'd say they should try having an orgy once and while, but could you imagine a bunch of religious people having an orgy. It'd be like trying to eat as much plain toast as you could with nothing to drink."

"Thanks for the metaphor but-" started Mathew before the witch interrupted.

"It was a simile."

"*But*, I still don't understand why you thought running everything would make you happy."

"Part of it was pressure from my mother, family legacy and all. Don't even get me started on my mother. She once-"

"I have heard," said Alteem. "More than any person should ever have to hear about your mother. We've been through a lot on this journey. This is a good moment to relax as we near our destination. Let's take it."

Chapter 24

The celebration started in the late evening. The sun had already dipped below the mountains, creating a halo of red light around them and a vague shadow across the valley. Bonfires sprouted up creating pockets of light that highlighted the figures moving about.

Food was set out in large bowls with tables and chairs scattered everywhere. Out came large drums whose beats echoed through the valley and through the bodies of those gathered. Voices were raised in song and bodies began to move in rhythmic patterns, dancing along with the flames.

Alteem wandered around. He'd grabbed himself a bowl of grains, with some fruits mixed in and sauce sprinkled on. It was much sweeter than he was used too, and though pleasant, its richness made it difficult for him to eat much.

He spotted Flamelash sitting alone, his eyes passively watching the event before him. Alteem moved beside him, and leaned against a building. "Why did you decide to come here?"

Flamelash looked up at him, the flames dancing across his eyes highlighted the redness in them. The bandits face gave away nothing. "I don't intend to stay."

"Then why come at all?"

"Because the others would not have if I didn't. My coming gave them permission to do what was in their hearts. I'll wait until they're settled and slip away."

"Then what?"

Flamelash looked away from him, his eyes fixing on one of the fires.

"I'd have never thought beastmen capable of this." Said Alteem.

"Neither I, tis not in their nature. It seems they are capable of going against it."

"Honey once tried to convince me even demons could be good if given the chance."

Flamelash glanced up at him out of the corner of his eye. "I'm $1/17^{th}$ demon."

"I'm sorry I- wait, $1/17^{th}$?"

"It's a complicated lineage."

"But, that's not even possible."

"It's a very complicated lineage."

"Could you explain it?"

"Not to you," Flamelash said, picking up a round piece of fruit from a nearby bowl. He bit into it and the juice poured out over his fingers and chin.

"I'm sorry if I upset you, but, demons are demons. They are evil incarnate, nothing can change that."

Flamelash paused in his eating of the fruit. "Am I, like you?" He said. "Is that what I sound like to other people when I talk about beastmen?"

"You said it yourself, things have a nature to them. That's just a fact."

"I am like you." Flamelash got to his feet. "I need to think about some things."

Alteem was left briefly alone, wondering if someone who was part demon was more capable of personal growth than he was. Then wondering if him thinking the demon part would make it harder for a person to have personal growth was part of the problem.

Honey burst out of group of people and was right next to him in a flash. She radiated heat, energy, and excitement. Her skin shimmered a little in the firelight from sweating. "Alteem, are you having a good time?"

"I might be too old to enjoy celebrations like these anymore."

"I'm older than you."

"Maybe I'm just too boring then."

"I guess that makes sense. You are boring."

"A little, perhaps."

"A lot, definitely."

"You're exaggerating."

"No really, what is your personality."

Alteem thought for a moment, "I'm good."

"And?"

Alteem paused another moment. "I...brood."

"That's not a personality trait."

"I'm a very serious person."

"Yup, serious and brooding, and that's about it."

"I have a deep emotional conflict."

Honey rolled her eyes. "Lot's of people do. It might seem like it makes you more compelling, but without any more substance than that it's just superficial drama."

"Fine, I'm just a blank slate with no real personality."

"Maybe think about getting one. You're a hero prince who suffered horrible tragedy, and the peasant housewife who married you is more interesting."

"Anyway," said Alteem eager to change the subject. "I'm surprised you haven't used your magic to enhance the celebration."

"I made cake," Honey said smiling. "It's made out of peace and har-mony."

"What's that taste like?"

"Mmmm, like melted chocolate and raspberry cream."

"What's chocolate?"

"You've never had chocolate?"

"No."

"Has Alma ever had chocolate?"

"No, I don't think so."

"I need go right now. I have to make sure she has a piece." Honey darted off back into the crowds, disappearing as quickly as she'd arrived. She weaved through the dancing crowds with uncanny agility. She climbed atop one of the bonfires hoping to get a better look at the crowd. Her clothes quickly lit on fire and she remembered what she'd forgotten in her excitement. That clothing was not as fire proof as she was.

Being naked didn't bother her, it was a party after all, but if people saw her hair it would be a dead giveaway to her identity. She spared a brief moment to morn her clothes, she had liked them, even if they weren't her usual style. Then she asked someone nearby where she might find some spare clothes. The person eyed her with some concern, as she might, given all her clothes were on fire. They were made of magic, so they'd last longer than normal clothes, but they'd turn to ash and fall away eventually.

The woman pointed her to a house that had some cloth in it she could use to cover up. Honey bolted to the house. The crowd parted easily for her, not wanting to catch fire themselves. Once at the entrance she discarded what remained of her clothes in a single motion before entering. The clothes floated gently to the floor before burning out a few moments later.

Inside it was clearly a place they stored cloth. Piles of it lined the walls, neatly organized in different colors. She could probably use her magic to fashion herself up something nice in a few minutes, but she didn't want to miss any more of the celebration. She wrapped herself up in particularly large piece of red cloth. Folding and tying it up in strategic place she grabbed another piece of cloth and wrapped up her hair in it.

Rushing back outside she resolved to simply ask around for Alma. No one knew who she was, and Honey wasn't getting anywhere. There weren't that many humans around, and only a couple of them were female. She decided to just ask if anyone had seen a human female. Using this, slightly more practical method, she quickly located Alma, who was sitting on a bench tapping her foot.

"Alma!" Honey said, rushing over to her.

"Honey, you've, changed clothes."

"Yeah, I accidently lit the others on fire. Listen, have you ever had chocolate?"

"What's that?"

"I don't believe this, how have you lived until now?"

"Through hardship and struggle, brought on in large part because most the earth was poisoned with evil magic and the lands covered in darkness making it near impossible to grow food."

"Okay fine, I can see how that would make it difficult to get chocolate. Also, sorry, again. But you have to come with me and try some of the cake I made."

"I'm alright just sitting here, Honey."

"But...cake."

"I suppose I can try some, if it will make you happy."

"No," said Honey. "It will make you happy, and also me, so, yes."

The witch took Alma by the hand and led her to the cake tables. "I've never seen so much cake." Said Alma.

"There's a lot of people here. I wanted there to be enough for everyone. It did take all afternoon, even with magic."

The cake itself spanned five long tables, its colors a white and black marble. Even at its size, nearly half had already been eaten.

Pieces of cloth were used to distribute it, and Honey grabbed one. Placing a piece of cake on it she handed it to Alma.

Alma picked a small chunk of the cake with her fingers. Popping it in her mouth she began to chew, then slowly sank to her knees. A single tear rolled down her cheek. "This is the greatest thing I have ever tasted."

"I know," said Honey.

"It's better than sex."

"Really?" Said Honey. "I'm going to have to have a talk with Alteem."

"That might not be the best idea."

"Alma, I was right about the cake, I'm right about this too."

Mathew walked up to them, a drink in his hand.

"Are you drinking?" asked Alma.

"No," Mathew lied. "There's no alcohol in this. What are you two talking about?"

"Alteem needs to step up his sexual prowess with your mother. Why are two looking at me like that? What did I do now?"

"It's alright," Alma said, Mathew offering a hand to help her get back to her feet. "You go back to enjoying yourself."

"Aren't you going to dance?" Honey asked.

"I'm too old for dancing."

The witch frowned. "I'm older than you, and if there's something else my apprentice can learn from me, it's that you're never too old for dancing. If you'll excuse me, I have to go give Alteem a detailed lecture about sex."

"Well then, Mother," said Mathew extending a hand towards Alma. "Shall we dance?"

"You have been drinking." Said Alma.

"Perhaps a little."

Honey came bounding next to Alteem. "We need to talk about sex?"

"Good," said Alteem. "That's exactly what I wanted to talk to you about."

"Really?"

"Yes, Flamelash says he's 1/17th demon."

"Yes."

"I've been trying to figure it out, but it's impossible."

"Demon's don't all reproduce in the same manner mammals do."

"Explain it to me."

"I can try, but I don't think you'll understand."

"Just try."

Flamelash wandered through the shadows. The darkness was more comfortable to him than the light. People couldn't see you in the darkness. Even if no one here was likely to judge him, the familiarity of the shadows still gave him comfort.

"Why do they call you Flamelash?" Asked a high voice just inside the firelight. A young beastgirl stood watching him. Her catlike eyes glowing.

"Because of my red eyes." Flamelash lied, using one of his fingers to point to his eyes.

The girl frowned, then ran back off to the dancing.

"Why do they really call you that?" Asked Tumon, who came from the darkness as well.

"Spying on me?"

"You've spent a great deal of time on your own, I was concerned."

"I have always preferred myself as company."

"So it is for some, but you did not answer my question."

Flamelash looked up at the moon. "I was born a slave, long before the witch enslaved the world, and then ended all slavery. All I ever knew of the world was the mine I was forced to work in. Even as a child, they made us play games that was just work in disguise. Moving rocks around, and climbing into tight spaces. As I grew older, life grew cruel. The taskmaster had a whip whose end burned with magical flame. It let him whip his slaves longer since it cauterized the wounds, stopping the bleeding. They would only pass out if the pain became too much, and he enjoyed finding out what was too much.

"One day I caused a great accident, which put work back several months. He strung me up and whipped me for as much as I could stand several days in a row until my back was nothing but burns and scars.

"After I was released to work again, I realized I no longer cared if I lived or died. The only reason I had any strength at all was because of my demon blood. I walked up to the taskmaster as he whipped another, and grabbed the whip at the flame." Flamelash took one of the gloves of his hand revealing the scars from burning. "I wrapped it around his neck and strangled him, his neck burning as he died. I still remember the smell. The guards attacked and I used the whip to fight them off. I meant to die there, killing as many of them as I could. But the slaves rose up, killing their masters.

"Even though I led them to their freedom, they still would not accept me because of my demon heritage. I was free, but still trapped by a world that would not accept me. The name Flamelash stuck, even though I destroyed the whip."

"So," said Tumon. "Because violence was the path to your freedom, it was how you learned to get what you want."

Flamelash met Tumon's owl eyes. "Yes."

"I was the same once."

"What I really came to want," said Flamelash. "Was to create a place where everyone would be accepted. I did create such a place, but we were always desperate, always moving, always had enemies nipping at our heels. Yet here it is, that place that I dreamed of. Now that I am here, all I want to do is leave."

"Violence is lined across your soul. It has infected you, as it was with me. How impossible it feels to live without it when it has lodged itself into the core of your being."

"How did you do it?"

"At first not at all. I did not want to let go. I rejected the peace, and mocked and scorned those who created it. I feared it might make me soft, or that I might not be anyone at all without it. It was what I knew, how to kill, how to fight, how to survive. Then one day, I started to let go, just little at a time. Then came a time, without even realizing it, when I'd let it all go. It did make me soft, but I did not disappear. I was still me, but a new me, soft, and kind, and warm. That is this place."

Flamelash nodded, turning back to his thoughts.

Tumon took the cue, and left the bandit to himself once more. He wandered about the celebration. Spotting Alteem talking to Kaytee he walked over to them.

"The Brazog demons breed in groups of five or more at a time." Said Alteem.

"Yes." Said the witch.

"But which one of them has the baby?"

"They all do."

"That doesn't make any sense."

"I told you you wouldn't understand!"

"I hope," said Tumon. "You're both enjoying the celebration."

"Yes," said the witch. "Did you have some of the cake?"

"It was very excellent."

"I know, I'm very good."

"You've changed clothes I see."

"I lit the other ones on fire."

"On purpose?"

"No, didn't seem like that sort of party."

Tumon frowned at the witch. "You must have had some interesting parties in your time."

"They never quite lived up to what I was looking for."

"What was missing from them?"

"Happiness."

"Happiness?"

"Yes," She said, her gaze dropping and growing sad. "There was always plenty of pleasure at my parties, but not happiness."

"I think I understand. Are you happy now?"

"I think so."

"You don't know?"

"I've never been happy before. I'm not sure what it feels like."

"Surely you must have had some happy times as a child."

"You didn't know my mother?"

"What about your father?"

"She killed my father after procreation. Family tradition."

"I see, would you like to talk about your mother?"

"Yes, yes I would."

"I have to go." Said Alteem, getting up and leaving. He wandered around, feeling uneasy surrounded by his hated enemies. Violent monsters, so had been every beastmen he'd ever known. They came down from the mountains only to kill and steal. Yet here they were, living peacefully. Alteem would not have believed it unless he saw it for himself. The world he knew was gone, destroyed in terror and burned to the ground.

In all those years, alone in a dark prison, he'd never have dreamed a new world could come from all the terrible things that happened. For the first time he was starting to believe the new world could be better than the last one. That their quest really could stop wars from breaking out again. He saw Alma, dancing with her son, and he smiled.

"May I cut in?" Alteem asked.

"Of course," Mathew said. "Gives me a chance to grab another drink."

"Not too much," said Alma as Alteem put his hands around her. "He's homesick. All this time he's wanted to get away and see the world. I think now he realizes how much that little corner of the world meant to him."

"What about you?" Asked Alteem.

"I never wanted more than my own tiny insignificant life. Honey talks of all these worlds and places, and it makes me realize how small we all are, but it doesn't bother me. I never wanted to be more than small. Now, I've seen wonderful and terrible things. I'm an apprentice to the most powerful witch who ever lived. Nothing will probably come from it, but I like it. When this is all over, I think I want to stay with her. I want to see more, all those things I never even dreamed existed."

"I hope you'll visit often."

"You won't come with?"

"I've seen too many things. I miss my school, I miss my students. They were a lot easier to manage than my current one. I don't think she needs me much anymore. I'm not the hero prince anymore. I'm just a teacher, and it's brought me a great deal more joy than being a prince ever did."

Flamelash saw honey talking to Tumon and he walked over.

"That was the fifth time my mother sent me to hell to punish me." Said Honey.

"But you were making friends there." Said Tumon.

"As much as you could call them friends, comrades would be a better word. We really razed some hell together, which was impressive since we were already in hell."

"Do you think maybe you acted out because home was more of a hell for you than actual hell?"

"You know, I might have."

"Excuse me," said Flamelash. "I think I would regret going through a celebration like this without dancing. Would you care to dance?" He extended a hand to Honey.

She frowned at him. "Why me?"

"Because I've always loved you and only now found the courage to say so."

"No really, why?"

"Then how about because I simply wish to dance with a beautiful woman."

"No."

"Because I want to dance with an old friend."

"We were never friends, but fine."

"You flatter me."

Honey took his hand, and he led her into a crowd. Slipping a hand around her waist, Flamelash started to sway to the music.

"This is awkward." Said Honey. "You're too tall."

"You're too short. Do you like being that way?"

"I didn't have a choice in the matter."

"Couldn't you have magiced yourself up a few inches?"

"Healing people is one thing, completely reconstituting a person is something different."

"I've seen you wipe out armies with a wave of your hand, but growing a bit taller is too difficult."

"I've seen you kill a person, but I've never seen you bring one back to life. Destruction is easy, but I would have to rearrange every atom in my body to make myself taller. Unless I just made my legs longer, but then I'd be all out of proportion."

"And you are so well proportioned."

"Exactly."

Flamelash laughed. "You've changed a great deal, but you're still you after all."

"Why did you join me, all those years ago?"

"I saw what happened to those who didn't."

"Everyone saw what I did to my enemies, not everyone joined me. You joined early, when I might have still been stopped."

"Could you have been stopped?"

"I might be able to face an army alone, but an army has no reason to face me on my own. I could have simply rode around terrorizing people, but what good would that have done. Didn't you ever wonder why I had an army in the first place? I needed people to hold land, once I was gone. I wanted to rule the world. If people had taken out all my followers I'd have been forced to give up."

"I joined you at first to try and stop you."

"You meant to betray me?"

"I'd heard rumors of an item that could kill you hidden away in a dungeon on top of the highest mountain. It was said only the worthy could pass the trials and wield it. I didn't think whatever the trials were they would deem a part demon worthy. I sent some of my best men to find it, hoping if they did, they could use it on you easily if I was close to you. They never returned."

"I started those rumors. I also built the dungeon."

"You built a dungeon containing an item that would stop you?"

"No, there was no item. It was just a series of monsters and traps to kill people. I put clues to all the puzzles around the dungeon, but then none of them actually had solutions. If people put in a code, or aligned some disks or whatever it would just kill them regardless of the arrangement. I figured if all the heroes went looking for this item instead of trying to stop me it would increase my chances."

"You always were a clever bitch."

"The cleverest," Honey smiled.

"At one point I thought about trying to be your consort."

"Really?"

"No one else was vying for the job. You seemed lonely, I thought perhaps it would be better to rule by your side than under you. The fact you're inhumanly beautiful didn't hurt either."

"What changed you mind?"

"I realized I would never be your equal. You outclassed me in every way. Not once did you ever look at me with a hint of maybe in your eyes."

"I don't know," she said eyeing him. "You might have had a shot, like you said, no one else wanted the job. I was very lonely, and it wasn't easy to meet people in the position I was in."

"I also was a little terrified of what you might have been like in the bedroom."

"I have had great deal of angry sex, but no one's died yet. Not since I've been sober anyway."

"I was glad you took my advice about the drinking."

"Thank you for that, things were getting a little out of control."

"More than a little."

"Those poor emus."

The music began to pick up, the voices and drums moving faster. They separated, but didn't stop dancing together. Honey's movement picked up pace to keep in time with the drums, bouncing rhythmi-cally, getting lost in the sound and the motion. She heard Flamelash say something, but she couldn't make it out. He grabbed her arm firmly to stop her from bouncing. "Your hair." He said.

She reached up, but was too late, the cloth holding her hair up slipped away. The multi-colored locks came loose down her back. Only one person in the world had hair like her, and everyone could recognize it at a glance.

The witch froze, feeling gaze after gaze turn to her. Whispers and murmurs replaced the sound of song. The silence spread across the celebrations, until even the drums stopped. She was on one of the lower divides so people from all around were staring down at her. She looked around at them all, faces she'd seen so many times before. They hated her, they judged her, and the worst of it was knowing how de-served it was.

Time froze for her, and she had no idea how long she stood there when there was hand on her shoulder. She looked at its owner, Tumon smiled down at her.

"Everyone is welcome here," he whispered to her. Then he turned to the crowd, his voice weighted with wisdom. "Everyone is welcome here."

Their faces softened, then they smiled and it was repeated across the valley. "Everyone is welcome here."

Honey felt tears come to her eyes, as she was suddenly overwhelmed with a feeling. She felt happy, she was certain of it, this is was what happiness felt like. So she did the only that seemed sensible in the moment, she ran away from it.

Chapter 25

Alma wandered through the dark parts of the city, torch in hand. The sounds of celebration had resumed, but they'd grown distant now. Finding Honey might have been difficult, except the persistent sound of sobbing that guided the way. The torchlight eventually found a huddled figure.

"Sorry," Honey said. "I probably upset everyone."

"Don't worry, the party goes on without us, it always does."

"It was a stupid thing to do."

"No," said Alma. "You experienced something you never experienced before. Even if something good happens, the unfamiliar can be terrifying. Sometimes it being a good unfamiliar makes it even more terrifying."

"It was everything I ever wanted, to be accepted, to be welcome somewhere. I didn't think there'd ever be place left on the planet I'd find myself welcome again. I don't deserve it, to be folded back into the warmth of humanity and companionship."

"Deserve? Perhaps not, or perhaps so, I don't know. I can't say who deserves anything. Deserve so often doesn't matter in life, and people are only concerned about it when they don't get what they think they deserve. It seems so easy for people to judge you as terrible, but I wonder about how many others, if they had your powers and gifts, would have done much the same, or worse. Of those, how many would have acknowledged their wrongdoing and tried to become good? Who knows, who ever knows? If there's one thing I do know, it's that others don't know as much as they're pretending.

"Stop worrying so much about whether or not you should be allowed to be happy, just be glad you've been lucky to have the opportunity. You know, I'm so glad I met you. I really didn't know what to think when Alteem first brought you home. Here you were, this terrifying legend, the stuff of nightmares. The longer you were around, the more I realized you were just as frightened of living as the rest of us, just as lost. You were larger than life, but so small, and you took me on an adventure I never dreamed of. I'm so ordinary, but you've transformed life into something I never imagined it could be."

"You're not ordinary," said Honey. "I doubt if I searched the whole world over I wouldn't meet another person who'd show me the kindness you have. I was alone, I had nothing and no one, and you let me into your home. If anyone transformed anyone's life, you transformed mine. You showed me what it meant to be kind, to show compassion for those the world said deserved none. I've never met someone so extraordinary, and I've been to many worlds."

"Let's go back now," said Alma.

"Okay."

They walked back to the party together. After they arrived, Honey sought out some drinks, her throat feeling raw from her crying. She spotted Mathew near some. Walking over, she grabbed one of the drinks and downed it as quickly as she could.

"I thought you didn't drink alcohol." Said Mathew.

The witch looked at him, her eyes growing wide with a sudden terror. "I thought you said there wasn't any alcohol in this."

"I was just kidding."

"Oh," said Honey. "Ooooooooh. This is bad."

Chapter 26

Honey woke up. The first thing she noticed was the terrible headache that felt as if it split her top to bottom. The second thing she noticed was that she was completely naked. The third thing she noticed was that she was sticky all over.

A moan came next to her. She looked over to see Mathew, just as naked as her, lying on the ground. They were outside, next to a pond that was fed by a trickling waterfall. His eyes opened, and he saw her. Looking around, he sat up and took in their surroundings. Then, he looked back at her, then back at himself, then back at her. "We... didn't, do anything did we?"

"The last thing I remember is taking a drink," said Honey. "But, based on the soreness of certain areas, I'd guess real serious hate sex was going on."

"Oh no. No, no, no, no, no. This is the worst thing that could have happened."

"That's hurtful." Said Honey, getting to her feet, small patches of dirt stuck to her.

"Where are we?"

"I know as much as you." Honey licked a non-dirt covered part of herself. "Are you sticky, because I'm covered in honey."

"Yes," said Mathew.

"Then we definitely had sex."

199

"Please stop saying that."

"So...you want to go again?"

"What?"

"Have sex."

"Why would we do that?"

"We already did, don't you want to know how it was?"

"No, I don't want to know anything about it. I didn't want to do it in the first place."

"Clearly you did, otherwise you wouldn't have."

"I was drunk."

"Come on, I'm gorgeous, some part of you must want me." Honey gestured along her body.

"If you'll shut up, I'll admit you're pretty, even if the rest of you is loathsome."

"Soooo, round two? Or, maybe three, or four, or five, no way of knowing really."

"I will never have sex with you again."

"If you're going to have to live with the guilt for the rest of your life, you might as well be able to remember the fun part."

"Why do want to have sex so bad?"

"Because its sex. You don't need a reason to want to have sex."

"This is not at all how I imagined my first time."

"Wait! What?"

"Nevermind." Mathew turned away from her.

"But...you went to university."

"It was an all-male university?"

"So."

"So I'm straight."

"So...it's university."

"Just forget it."

"Buuuut, if you can't remember your first time, doesn't that make you all the more curious as to what it was like."

Mathew looked at the witch, "If we did, you couldn't tell anyone, ever."

"Only if you promise not to hold back on the spankings."

"Spankings?"

"Of course," She said pouting. "I'm a very naughty little witch."

They heard the sound of a horse galloping towards them. Alteem and Alma emerged into their clearing a few moments later.

"Alteem, Alma!" Honey said. "Great to see you, but could you come back in, say, two hours."

"No!" Shouted Mathew. Then he paused and looked at the witch. "Two hours?"

"Magic," Said honey, smiling an innocent smile that was ill suited to her mischievous face.

Mathew thought for a moment. "No," he said.

"Well if I'm not getting laid again I'm washing this honey off."

Alteem regarded them with a strange look as he dismounted the horse. "We've been looking for you for two weeks. What happened?"

The witch paused on her way to the pond. "Two weeks? I didn't, do anything did I?"

Alteem helped Alma off the horse. "You started a sex cult that spanned a few towns. They were-"

"I don't want hear any details." Honey interrupted. "Just answer one question, cannibalism or no cannibalism?"

Alteem stared at her for a full minute before answering, slowly. "No cannibalism."

The witch let out a sigh of relief. "Thank goodness." She stepped into the pond and sunk down into it. "Good news though, eh Mathew. If we started a sex cult I might not have been your first time."

Mathew looked quickly at his mother then looked away. "I should get clean."

"The last people who saw you said you headed off naked this way," said Alma. "And that you were both covered in honey. So we brought you some clothes."

"No need," said Honey. She began to rise slowly out of the water. As she did so the water clung to her, and transformed into loose cloth the same deep blue color of the pond. The dress that formed hung loose around her. The cloth itself was so thin it barely seemed there. As the witch moved it would occasionally brush against her body and reveal her curves. The sleeves hung down all the way to her hands, and part of them extended just past her hands coming to a point. The light shimmered off it, just as if it were the water, and it slid around her, frictionless, as she moved. The whole process took several minutes.

"I need the clothes," said Mathew, taking them from Alma. "Thank you."

"Fortunately you two headed in the right direction." Said Alteem. "We're only a few days more from our destination."

"How about that?" Said Honey. "Everything worked out for the best. Maybe now I'm not evil anymore I should go on drunken binges more often."

Alteem walked up to her, crossed his arms and looked down at her. "Cannibalism?"

"Maybe not."

"After Mathew's finished we should get going. I heard rumors that different leaders are marshaling armies. We're running out of time." Said Alteem.

"Time is always running out for something." Said Honey.

"But in this case time is running out to stop war from breaking out across the globe."

"Blah, blah, blah. You're like a broken record."

"A what?"

"Nevermind. Let's just go."

"But," said Mathew. "I'm not done cleaning off the honey." Alteem glanced at him. "The food, not...not her."

"Hurry up then," said Alteem.

After Mathew finished, the group continued on its way. A few days of camping, and they were approaching the gates of the city of Melscen, or what used to be. The witch had destroyed most of it in her conquest. Grand golden stone walls had once stretched fifty feet high, now they were mostly rubble. Once one of the proudest fortifications ever built, scavengers searched the ruins for any chunks that could still be useful. It's massive gate of steel that had taken forty men to open and close, was now just part of the road.

"This place was really fun to destroy." Said Honey.

Everyone looked at her.

"I am sorry about it, but I'd be lying if it wasn't my favorite part. Ah, you should have seen it in its glory. Gleaming buildings that reached for the sky, like a hundred penises."

"What?" said Alma.

"The buildings looked like penises, girthy penises, but there's nothing wrong with that. Then I brought it crashing down. A dirge of dicks, thundering into the ground, causing the earth to shake." Honey drew in a deep breath. "It felt so good."

"This is too weird," said Alteem. "I'm just going to keep going. Shouldn't you cover up your hair?"

"No more disguises. It's time I faced the world as myself again."

"Are you sure that's really a good idea here, given the avalanche of cock that occurred on your last visit."

"Ha, good one, but seriously, whatever the consequences, if I am to redeem myself, then I must do it as...myself. I should've practiced this moment, I bet I could have come up with a better line. If only I hadn't gotten distracted with that drunken binge."

"Give it some thought," said Alteem. "I'm sure you'll get another chance to deliver it."

They moved toward the city, crossing over the door which worked its way deeper into the road each day as more people walked over it.

Inside people had made houses out of the ruins. The former buildings had been large enough that people just claimed a few rooms for themselves. Even the ruins could be up to three stories high, and people just piled up stones to block off doors and made a space for themselves.

Even with all that had happened in the world, Melscen remained a populated urban center. So much so, that no one even noticed the witch, because no one ever bothered to look at anyone else.

"Excuse me," said Mathew to someone passing by, but they ignored him. He made another attempt, and was likewise ignored. Turning to the party he asked, "How are we supposed to find Sergei like this?"

"I could get people's attention." Said Honey.

"Whatever you're talking about, no." said Alteem. "Doesn't he work at the local university?"

"Yes," said Mathew. "If we can find that, we can find him."

"Where might it be?" Asked Alma.

"Now that I think of it," Said Honey. "You haven't been practicing your cosmos breathing. Wait, what happened to the cart?"

"We left it." Said Alma.

"And the shrubbery?"

"That too."

"How could you?"

"The cart was powered by your magic. What were we supposed to do with it?"

"I see your point." Said Honey, her shoulders slumping. "It is dangerous to leave a vortex of magic just lying around. I'll have to make a mental note to take care of it once we've solved the whole war thing."

"Which brings us back to the university." Said Mathew.

"We could just wander around and hope we find it." Said Alma.

"But what if it looks like everything else?" Said Honey.

"It doesn't, it was built after your rampage across the world." Said Mathew

"How do you know that?"

"Because you built them all, near the end of your reign."

"That's right, I did, didn't I? I forgot all about that. It wasn't really me though. I wasn't trying to be a good ruler all of the sudden. Yes it was my idea, but I just wanted to stop everyone from nagging. Always the nagging, they never shut up, every day, all the time." Honey rubbed her temples. "I'm getting a headache even remembering."

"We just look for the one building that's different then." Said Alteem. "We'll split up and meet back at the gates at midday."

"I should've built information centers people could go to." Said Honey. "Seems like the sort of thing that would be useful to people coming into a town they're not familiar with."

"Okay," Said Alteem. "Everyone be careful, and stay safe. If a place gives you a bad feeling, it's probably for a reason. Let's go."

Chapter 27

Mathew wandered through the city, gleaming stones still lay strewn about next to gleaming walls. He couldn't help but wonder what this place must have looked like in its prime. They had the best university in the world, because before the witch had built universities, they'd prized science and art. It was no accident that the person who'd written the greatest pamphlet ever conceived had come from here. Now Mathew was here too, after such a long journey.

He saw a sign that read 'museum'. The building looked as much like any other building, mostly destroyed but with a few stories still standing. As much as he knew he was supposed to be looking for the university, he had to go in.

The first room had a mural painted all along the walls. It was a view of the city from the outside, only inverted since the view surrounded him. 'Wow,' he thought. 'The buildings really did look like penises.' He couldn't help but wonder if they had known, or if somehow, they never saw it.

A desk sat at the end of the room. A sign asking for donations hung from it. It seemed strange to leave precious artifacts and artwork unattended, but then perhaps people in the town cared enough about these things to leave them alone.

After dropping a few coins in the basket, Mathew moved through the left door. Inside were several paintings, a couple of which he'd heard of, but most were unfamiliar. He moved through the museum, finding artwork, and sculptures, and artifacts of old. Then he came across a piece that caught his attention. It was of the witch.

The painting covered the whole wall. The witch stood just off center, purple energy cracking and swirling around her. An army of black silhouettes flanked her on the right, and to the left was the city of Melscen, it's buildings crumbling as the witch's magic tore through them. It was a masterpiece, top to bottom. The lighting was perfect, stark and strong, in all the right places. The structure perfect, shapes showing a language even beyond what could easily be seen on the surface. The pain of the city glimpsed perfectly without even seeing a single person inside. But what really caught his attention, was how perfect the witch was painted.

Every detail was accurate, every strand of her hair's color, every curve, even the slight discoloration of her eyes. Even more impressive, was the look on her face. It twisted in vicious glee, but buried deep inside, profound sadness. A sorrow guarded by endless walls built over multiple lifetimes. For all the times Mathew had seen this face, this was the first time he really looked at Honey.

"I saw her once," came a voice from his side.

Mathew jumped a little. He'd been so engrossed in the painting he hadn't noticed the woman come up by his side.

"She wandered through the city after destroying it." The woman was short, and thin to the point of malnourishment. She had a crutch under her left arm, and it was clear something was wrong with her left leg. There was a quirky sort of attractiveness to her face, as if all the parts were pretty on their own, but didn't quite fit together right.

"Did you paint this?" He asked her.

"Yes."

"It's perfect."

She smiled, "It was commissioned by the Mayor, but it was something I'd wanted to do ever since that day."

"You must have a great memory to capture her likeness so perfectly."

"Have you seen her too?"

"I've seen more of her than I ever would have liked."

"I wonder what she's like, as a person. Would she be terrifying, or calm, like a predator you know could strike at any moment."

Mathew tried not to laugh, but failed. The woman shot him a queer look. He couldn't help but think back to the first time Alteem brought Honey to the table. At that time she had seemed like a predator that could strike at any moment. He'd grown so used to her presence that it was easy to forget she could kill him on a whim. Perhaps it was because he knew she never would, not anymore. Honey wasn't like that anymore. She'd grown, and learnt, but Mathew still couldn't get past what she'd been.

"You think it's funny I want to meet the witch? Most people do."

"Sorry, it's not that, it's just. I've met her, she's not what you'd think."

"Really, what *was* she like?"

Mathew thought of the best way to describe her. "Annoying, but in a weirdly charming way."

The woman frowned at him, but accepted the answer. "I was surprised how beautiful she was. I thought someone so evil must be ugly. At first I thought she was a spirit, that I'd died in the destruction and she was some unearthly thing come to take me to the afterlife. She looked so sad, and then she smiled. A person, bloody and dying, dragged themselves out of the ruin, cursing her. The witch cackled and killed him with barely a motion of her finger. What do you think happened to her?"

"She renounced her cruelty and malice, and set out a quest to become good."

The woman laughed, "Like that could ever happen? It would be pretty amazing, though, wouldn't it? Imagine the good she could do with her power."

"She could heal hundreds of people all at once. She could halt floods, prevent dams from breaking, and turn her former dark minions to good. Without even blinking an eye she could grow fields of crops to feed the hungry, stop wars, and make monsters reform."

"She could do anything."

"No, she couldn't bring back the millions of people she killed. She can't undestroy cities and lives. Nor can she give back the time to those enslaved. Her sins cannot be undone, no matter what else she does."

"I suppose your right. It's just a dream anyway. It's not like she's just going to walk in here and heal my leg."

"Was it hurt when the city was destroyed?"

"Yes, a large stone fell on it, and it didn't heal right."

"Then she owes it to you. Come on, follow me."

Chapter 28

Alma walked down the street. Part of her wondered what the place looked like when it was whole, but it was still remarkable to see in the state it was. It was a city so grand, people could even live in its ruins. Even the rubble gleamed.

How could people spend every day in such a place and not be in constant awe of the world around them. She thought back to her own small corner of the world. It was beautiful too, in a different way. Grand fields and open air that stretched out in all directions. She'd grown so used to it, she'd forgotten what a beautiful place it was. It happened to everywhere then, she guessed. What a waste, that the people who live in a place are the ones who often least appreciate it.

As she moved deeper into the city she saw gigantic cranes at work, lifting old stones up onto the ruins of the building. The cranes were so huge that it took a series of small machines working together to operate them. It was slow going, the first city must have been built over generations, and it would take generations to rebuild it. The city she was seeing now would be gone, and a new city would be here in its place. One day, that too would be gone, and the fact everything would be gone, just made it all matter that much more.

So it was with people too, she supposed. There was so many faces walking the streets. Each had a life Alma would know nothing about. We get used to people just like we get used to places, and we forget just how much they mean to us. One day they're there, and then they're gone, and it makes the time we have with them mean all that much more.

Their journey was coming to an end, but a part of her wanted it to go on forever. She'd found herself a part of this strange new family, long after she'd thought herself settled. She got to see her son every day, a thing she never thought would happen again. Then, she got to see a side of Alteem he'd once buried away.

Then, there was Honey, the lost soul who had shown up one day in her home. Alma had been too shocked at the time to be afraid. Alteem had been a legend. He'd come to them so haggard that she'd gotten used to the idea of him by the time she'd learned who he truly was. The witch, she was more than legend. She had changed the whole shape of the world. Nothing would ever be the same because of her. People told stories of the witch to frighten their children. The land still bared raw scars from the war she waged across the world. Countless died, most of whom never even to have the decency of a grave. There she was, sitting at the table, unlike anything Alma ever could have imagined.

The witch was not a monster, just a person as lost and confused as everyone else. She pretended to be fine like everyone else. She just wanted to figure out how to live, like everyone else. What was a person supposed to think when it turned out all the monsters in the world were just other people. Not twisted and broken creatures seeking to cause as much suffering and torment as they could, but just people. So Alma took pity on her, as a person, and look what it had done.

Turning a corner, Alma saw it. There was a building unlike any other, not in ruins, and made of wood instead of stone. She'd found the university.

Chapter 29

Alteem moved through the city, its crumbled buildings reminding him of his own ruined country. The whole thing made him feel slightly on edge. All the buildings here looked the same, the only distinguishing features their varied levels of ruination. It would be an easy place to get lost in.

The former prince stopped in his tracks, looked around, and realized he was lost. Even if he found the University, he doubted he could find it again. The best thing to do was just to walk in one direction until he found the wall, then he could follow the wall back to the gate.

He picked south, since it was the direction the gate was in, and would most likely bring him closest to it. After walking a good distance he came to a part of the city that grew increasingly empty. He knew from experience such places could be dangerous. Regretting not having a sword on him, Alteem took on a more confident stride. Predators could sense weak prey. He knew not to appear so.

Passing by several buildings, he saw neither person nor heard a sound. Perhaps he was just paranoid, giving the massive population reduction it wasn't unheard of for cities to have large sections abandoned. Melscen was unique in how packed it was, since its buildings had been reduced even more than its population. Still, even it wasn't completely immune to this new phenomenon.

Then, he heard the sound of voices. His guard went up. They were distant, but Alteem picked up a rock, just in case he needed something to defend himself with. As he moved the voices grew closer, and he considered changing course to avoid them. Curiosity got the better of him.

"Give it back." He heard someone say. Laughter was the response, then the sound of someone crying out in pain.

Alteem rushed towards it. If a person was in trouble, he was obligated to help. A couple of turns and Alteem saw three boys standing over a forth. One of the boys held a sword in his hand, and he kicked the boy on the ground.

"Enough." Said Alteem, he used his teacher voice on them.

They turned to look at him. "It's none of your business old man." Said the boy holding the sword. "Get out of here."

"Is that your sword?" Alteem said to the boy on the ground.

The boy nodded.

"It's mine now," said the leader.

"You will give it back, and you will leave him alone."

"Or what?"

"There is no 'or', that is what will happen."

The boys laughed at him. The leader pointed the sword at Alteem. "You think you can make me."

"I can," said Alteem, closing the distance between them. "But I don't want to. Wouldn't you rather do the right thing on your own?"

"You must crazy, or a drunk."

"I was a drunk once, and a prince before that, but now I am teacher."

"You think you can teach me something?"

"Yes," said Alteem, he pushed the sword out of the way and then seized the boy by his wrist. The other two ran away. Alteem moved the boys hand so it was next to the boy on the ground. "Give it back." The sword was dropped, the leader boy looking at him with a mix of fear and anger. "I know not your story, child, so I will not judge you. But I hope you realize one day that you do not have to act this way. Now go, leave him alone."

The boy ran as soon as Alteem released him. The child on the ground took the sword and got to his feet. "Thank you," he said.

"My name is Alteem, what's yours?"

"I'm Edgar."

"What's a boy doing with a sword?"

"It was my father's, he died. He used to be a guard."

"Were you trying to be a guard? Is that why those boys were bullying you?"

The boy looked away from him. "I thought I could scare them away with the sword, but they didn't think I would use it on them."

"It is unwise to hold a sword if you're unwilling to use it." Alteem said the words without thinking. They were something that had been drilled into him long ago. He had lived by them for many years, but they seemed wrong now. He felt he must amend the statement. "That is why it is unwise to hold a sword."

"Someone has to. There's bad people, someone has to stand up to them."

"You cannot kill your way to solving problems."

"I don't want to kill anyone. I just want to stop bad people from doing bad."

"Do you even know how to use that thing?"

"Swing it at people?"

"A sword is different than a stick," said Alteem. "With a stick you swing it at people, but with a sword you need to be slicing with it. It needs to cut its way through." The boy flinched a little at Alteem's words.

"Can you teach me?"

Alteem looked at the boy, and he thought of himself when he was younger. He had thought much the same, wanting to strike out and make the world a better place. The boy could be a hero. Another person willing to fight for what was right would not be a bad thing in the world. The prince had put down his sword, perhaps it was time for him to pass his training onto another. Then another thought entered his head. Alteem had known too many heroes, all dead now. He recalled his cousin's last desperate attempt to kill the witch. The world didn't need more corpses, and Alteem didn't need more lifeless faces to haunt his dreams on restless nights.

"I will tell you a story about a hero," said Alteem. "His name is Tumon."

Chapter 30

Honey was not used to walking around unnoticed. She'd been a bit nervous about removing her disguise, but in this place everyone was disguised. However well she knew loneliness, this was a strange new kind. To have a hundred people pass you in a moment, and have no one there at all.

Her eyes caught something she did not expect. As an immortal dimension hopping witch who'd been to heaven, hell, and all places in between, she wasn't used to being caught off guard. Someone, somewhere in the faceless, voiceless crowd, was wearing one of her dresses.

After shoving her way through, she found the person and managed to tap them on the shoulder. "Isn't that my dress?" Honey asked.

The person turned and looked at her, recognition dawning on their face, then horror, fear, terror, and other synonyms for those things. "S-sorry." They stuttered out before turning and running as fast as they could.

For a moment Honey was surprised at the reaction, then she remembered who she was. "Wait, you're wearing it all wrong." She called after the person. "Mortals have no proper sense of fashion." She murmured to herself.

Now she knew the dress was here it would be easy to locate. She'd made it with her own magic, finding it again across a short distance was no problem.

Not long after she found herself walking up a staircase. Once the staircase had been inside a building, but now it was outside broken off three stories up. Honey stopped and knocked on the door she found at the top. No one answered. She pushed the door to find it locked. With a flick of her wrist, she ripped the door off its hinges, and stepped inside. Then, she carefully placed the door back on their hinges and undid the damage.

Inside the person screamed and huddled in a corner, a kitchen knife clutched with white knuckles in their hand. "Please don't kill me." They said. "I'm sorry I took your dress."

"I'm not going to kill you, I don't do that anymore."

"Really?" The person looked around confused.

"Yes, really, and the knife wouldn't work on me anyway, so you can put it away."

The person slowly put the knife to their side, their voice still quivering. "Do you want your dress back?"

"No, no, I don't need it. I can make new dresses whenever I want. Like this one I made out of water, isn't it gorgeous?"

"It's very beautiful."

"Thank you, no one else said anything."

"What do you want?"

"To fix your dress, like I said, if you're going to wear it, you should wear it right. The hips are too wide, the waist to tight, and I don't know what's going on with the chest, but, it, is, not, working girl. Girl? Is it girl? What should I call you?"

"You can call me Erika, but I really haven't figured out the girl or boy question."

"No bother, the point is I'm going to make you look great in that dress."

"You really don't care about my gender?"

"Why would I?"

"Everyone else thinks I'm a freak."

"You can't be serious. There's disease, famine, pestilence and plague, earthquakes, starving children, war, ME, people must have more important things to worry about than your gender."

Erika shrugged.

"That's the stupidest thing I've ever heard. You know, you remind me of a half succubus, half incubus demon I dated briefly. Ah, they were the best of both worlds. Then they met another half succubus, half incubus demon who was male in all the parts they were female and female in all the parts they were male. Who was I to stand in the way of such a fated true love?"

Erika stared wide eyes at Honey. "Okay."

"Why did you take my dress?"

"It was so beautiful. I thought it could make me look beautiful."

"You thought my dress was beautiful? I mean, of course it is, but people so rarely say so. It *will* make you beautiful, we just have to make some adjustments. Up, stand up, no more cringing in the corner." The witch started to zap different parts of the dress with her magic. "Take in the hips, let out the waist, give us a nice smooth line going down here. Maybe add a slit, show off the legs, I can see someone works out. Fix the chest, let those subtle ruffles lay nice and flat. Form those shoulders to yours, and there, my work, as always, is perfect." With a wave of her hand the witch pulled a mirror out of stone. "What do you think, Erika?"

"Oh! I look beautiful."

"Of course you do, my fashion skills are literally magic."

"I feel beautiful too, and I don't think I've felt that way before." Tears appeared in Erika's eyes.

"Don't cry, you'll make me cry."

"It's just, no one's ever shown me such kindness before. I never thought it would come from a stranger."

"I know what you mean," The witch said, welling up. "The same thing happened to me, after all I'd done someone showed me kindness and it meant the world to me."

"Then you do know how I feel."

"I do, I really do."

Erika hugged the witch, and she hugged her back, and they cried together for as long as they needed to.

Chapter 31

Alma was the first to arrive at the gate, followed by Mathew.
"Who's this?" Alma asked, looking the woman up and down.

"Where's Honey?" Mathew asked.

"Who's this?" Said the woman.

"This is my mother," said Mathew. "Mother this is...I didn't get your name."

"No," said the woman, crossing her arms. "You didn't. Nor did I get yours."

Alteem arrived. "I wasn't able to find it. Who's this?"

"Who are you?" Asked the woman.

"I'm Alteem."

"Like the last prince of Ernloheim?"

"I'm not a prince anymore."

"By the gods, you really are him." The woman moved closer to Alteem. "People said you would return some day, but I waved it away as hopeful nonsense."

"No, I'm not returning, there's no return, no prophecies. We're looking for Sergei Haffleford."

"What for?" The woman crossed her arms.

"New nations are forming, and with them armies," said Mathew. "It's only a matter of time before war breaks out in order to establish new borders. We're hoping he'll have some idea of how to bring the nations together peacefully."

"And what makes *him* so special?"

"He wrote the treatise against the witch. He's the most brilliant person alive."

"Where is Honey?" Asked Alteem.

"I'm here, I'm here," said Honey. "Sorry, for the delay. I met the most wonderful person. I'm glad we came here, are we ready to go?"

"We haven't found Sergei yet." Said Mathew.

"I forgot all about that. Did someone else find the university?"

"I did," said Alma.

"Perfect, it all worked out yet. Who's this?"

The woman's skinned turned pale, her body stiffening, with a slight but controlled tremble. "I knew this day would come, when you'd finally show yourself. It was only a matter of time before you came to kill me. I wrote what I wrote, because it was right, because people needed to read those words. I believed in a new world, a better world for all people. I will not shirk, nor run, but stand firm and as bravely as I can against you. I'm sorry if your fragile ego couldn't handle being insulted, but know this, you can't kill your way to solving problems."

"I don't want to spoil your moment," said Honey. "But I have to ask again, who's this?"

"You didn't come here to kill me?" Asked the woman.

"I'm sorry, maybe if I knew who you were I would have?"

"You're Sergei," said Mathew. "Sergei Haffleford."

"This is always a problem with foreigners." Said Sergei. "Our alphabets a bit different here. Say it with me. Seer."

"Seer."

"Gee."

"Gee."

"E."

"E."

"Seergee'e" Said Sergei.

"Seergee'e, okay, I see the mistake." Said Mathew

"I hope you're not too disappointed I have a vagina."

"No, I, of course not. I think it's great. I mean, alphabets and all that."

"So now you know who I am." Sergei said to the witch. "What are you going to do?"

"I'm sorry," Said Honey. "I still don't know who are. We've been looking for you, but I didn't listen to the reason."

"I wrote a treatise against you, it was the most circulated pamphlet that's ever been written. I wrote about how government should be derived from the consent of the people. About how everyone has inalienable rights that if denied gives them the right to rebel against a tyrannical government. About how people have a right to an equal say in their own governance. There was a whole bunch of things about equality, and human rights, and democracy."

"I do vaguely remember people saying something about that when they deposed me."

"They say you shouldn't meet your heroes but maybe you shouldn't meet your villains either. I practiced that speech and everything."

"Really, being deposed was the best thing that ever happened to me. I hated ruling the world. It was the worst. My life's gotten so much better since then. Thank you, if you're the one responsible for it."

Honey embraced Sergei in a hug. The woman grew stiff, and gasped. When Honey released her, Sergei tenderly put weight on her leg, then stomped on the ground a couple of time. "You, you healed me." She said.

"I do that now, it's no big deal."

"You're the one that broke it in the first place." Said Mathew.

"Did I? I'm very sorry. It could have been worse. Alteem could tell you stories about how awful of a person I am. Was. Am? I'm a completely different person now, but I still did all those things. It's complicated. I renounced evil and I'm good now."

"That doesn't make any sense, people aren't just evil or good. Morality isn't black or white, there's-"

"We've been over the whole 'shades' thing. Really, it's not a good metaphor, people should stop using it."

Sergei looked around at all of them. "But, people don't just wake up one day and decide to completely change who they are. That doesn't happen, well it does, but no one follows through with it."

"That's not exactly the way it happened. It took a couple days."

"A couple of days, for the most evil person in the world to turn good?"

"They were busy days," Honey shrugged.

"Don't forget you spent several months lying in the ground in contemplation," Said Alteem.

"Right, so, there you go."

"Fine," Said Sergei. "Let's say I accept that you're good now, which I don't. What are you doing with the last prince of Ernloheim? He's your archenemy."

"Actually, my archenemy is a woman named Melissa. I don't want to talk about that bitch."

"We don't have time to explain everything," said Alteem. "I'm with her because I wanted to help her be a better person."

"How has that been going?" Asked Sergei.

"Mostly well, she has a strange obsession with baby murder."

"Babies are the worst." Said Sergei.

"Finally," said the witch. "Someone's on my side."

"I'm not in favor of murdering them," Said Sergei. "I just hate them."

"Damn, so close." Honey said, snapping her fingers.

"Now I'm going to have to think of some new last words."

"I said that to someone earlier today," said Alteim. "That you can't kill your way to solutions."

"Damn it, really? That's always happening when you're a writer. You come up with something brilliant and someone beats you to it. Well, good luck to all of you."

"You're leaving, we came to you for help." Said Mathew.

"You came to me because you thought I might know what to do, and I do. Right next to you, you have an all-powerful witch. She might be able to convince the new world leaders to come together in order to negotiate the new borders peacefully. People might be reluctant to trust her, if only you had one of her former enemies who's beloved by the world to vouch for her. Shit, you know who'd be perfect, the last prince of Ernloheim. The solution was with you all the whole time, isn't that special."

"Where are you going?"

"To run, to jump, to have sex in previously unattainable positions."

"Ooo," said Honey. "Can I come?"

"No you can't." Said Alteem. Then Sergei was gone.

"I don't feel special," said Mathew. "I just feel stupid for not figuring that out on our own."

"It's all about the journey," said Honey.

"Yeah," said Alteem. "It was a good journey.

Chapter 32

The party set up camp just outside the view of the city. "What are we going to do now?" Asked Mathew, as they sat around their campfire.

"We go home," Said Alteem. "I can write letters, and verify my identity from there. That should be enough to vouch for Honey."

"That's it, after all this, we just leave Honey to save the world on her own."

"I'm not going home," said Alma. "I want to stay with Honey, and keep being her apprentice. If that's okay with you Honey?"

"It's not like you've been the best apprentice." Said Honey. "You didn't even care we lost the shrubbery, but I can't say no to you Alma. Nothing would make me happier than to have you stay with me."

"Mom," said Mathew. "You're not coming home?"

"I'm sorry sweetie, but I've seen so much on this adventure, and I want to see so much more."

"Home won't really be home without you." Said Mathew.

"Mathew." Said Honey. "You're just going to have to get someone else to cook all your meals."

"She didn't cook all my meals."

"You were there all the time."

"Enough," said Alma. "This is our last night all together. Tomorrow we say goodbye, can't you two just get along?"

"I can if he can." Said Honey.

Mathew nodded. "I'm not sure how I thought adventures like this ended, but, it feels incomplete."

"The best adventures," said Alteem. "Are the ones you get to go home at the end of. Not all of them are like that, and not everyone always makes it to the end. I do understand what you mean. It always feels a bit sad at the end. Even in a happy ending there's some sadness, because it's over."

"Yeah."

"Not for all of us," Said Honey. "For some of us the quest will never end. Such is the consequences of our actions. The debt I incurred is not a depth, it is a void that can only be fed, but never filled. Still, there's happiness to be found along the way, and love, and friendship. All the things that not that long ago I thought beyond my reach forever. Thank you all for a chance undeserved, I promise I will not waste it."

The party talked a little more, and drifted off to sleep over time.

Honey woke first the next day, rubbing the sleep out of her eyes as she sat up. With a snap of her fingers the fire place roared to life again. She stretched out her hands and let it warm her. Eventually she was joined by Alteem, who dug out a pan and started making breakfast on the fire. Mathew came up next, his sleeping bag still wrapped around him.

"Go fetch Alma, foods nearly ready." Said Alteem.

Honey got up from the fire and knelt down were Alma lay. The witch whispered her name softly and shook her. A moment of silence followed, then a burst of magic. Purple whirled around Honey and Alma and then was gone as suddenly as it had appeared.

Alteem looked over at them, confused by the magic. They were both still, but for one difference. Honey's body moved slightly as she breathed, Alma's did not. Alteem stood up, knocking the pan over. Its contents spilling out onto the ground. He rushed over, Mathew following him. Dropping by Alma's side he looked at Honey. Her eyes were locked on Alma. Honey's mouth opened to say what Alteem already knew, but no words came out. His hand reached out and touched Alma's cheek. It was cold.

"No," said Mathew. "Mom." He tried to lift her up by the shoulders, but recoiled when her head rolled lifelessly. "It can't be. Not here, not now, not after everything." He stumbled back, then looked to Honey. Her eyes rose to meet his. "This is all your fault," he said, venom dripping from his voice. "She should have been home. She should have been living her peaceful life, not out having adventures. You killed her."

Honey tried to say something, but no words would come.

"Say something!" Mathew screamed at her, but she remained silent. His hand swung, coming near her cheek before a flash appeared and his strike rebounded. He clutched his hand, looked to Alteem, then Honey, then his mother. "I didn't..." He started to say, then stopped and ran.

Alteem tucked Alma's head back into a resting position and started to wrap her up in a cloth. "I'm sure Mathew will return to apologize," He said. "People grieve in different ways, sometimes in ways they regret."

Honey just looked back at Alma, kneeling next to her, unable to speak. Tears started to roll down her cheeks and she let out a soft sob.

"You've never lost someone you've loved before, have you?"

"I..." She managed to get out, quiet and weak. "I don't think I ever loved anyone before. I don't know if I even knew how. It's so awful. There's no magic to heal this sort of wound."

Alteem paused his work a moment to look Honey in the eyes. "We think, how can we go on without them, how can the world go on without them? Yet it does, and so do we. The world doesn't ever seem to really need any of us, despite the fact that it needs all of us."

"I thought I understood," Said Honey. "I thought I knew what I had done, but I was wrong. To think, I did this to so many. I cast this suffering on millions. I cracked open the world and from it bled the mourning cries of all its peoples as their dead lay broken in the ruins. Their loved ones were torn away from them screaming into slavery. Hearts broken, families shattered, this is my sin, and I shall drown in the weight of it. A storm of torment whirls around me, and it tears at every part of me. The pieces rip off of me, and fly away, I am lost."

Alteem looked at the witch, at Honeydrops. More than any other, he had suffered at the hands of this woman. Punishment was often what people wanted when they looked for justice. What he had wanted was not punishment, but for her to understand, really under-stand why she was so wrong. Now she did, it gave him no satisfaction. He just felt bad for her.

"Long ago," said Alteem. "We fought against each other in a differ-ent world. There is much evil that can be laid at your feet, but there was much evil in the world before you came along. History is filled with atrocities and unrepentant monsters. Innumerable ghosts wander the world waiting for justice that will never come. There is a question that has no right answer and no wrong answer. We must all face it again and again. I cannot absolve you of all you have done. All I can say is this, for my own part. I forgive the wrong that you have done me."

"No, don't say that," Honey turned away from him. "I don't deserve it."

"It is not your choice to make. After I lost everything I thought my life was over. Once freed, I could not imagine how I could go on. I came to a place, and met a woman. She was not a remarkable woman, but she became so to me, and to you. She gave us each new lives by sharing her life with ours." He knelt next to Honey, and em-braced her. She embraced him back, and began sobbing uncontrol-lably. "It is so unfair, that time keeps selfishly passing, heedless of our grief. There is still a task ahead of you. One that you must do. One that, quite frankly, you owe to the world. Mathew will return, and we'll bury her together, but you must go."

"No," said Honey. "She should be buried at home." Pulling herself away from Alteem, she pointlessly wiped away a few tears and whirled her hand in the air. A purple ribbon appeared and wrapped itself around Alma. "It will preserve her for the journey."

"Will you ever come to visit her?"

"Someday I shall perhaps, but I think I will be very busy as I have much to do."

"Goodbye." Said Alteem.

"Goodbye." Said Honey.

Epilogue

Never had such a group been assembled before. In a valley, surrounded by hills, several stone benches had been hauled in to seat the nearly thousand people who'd all come. They didn't really have a choice, only those who showed would have the protection of the witch against their enemies. Those who refused would forfeit the most powerful ally anyone of their world could have.

It had taken great deal of time for seating arrangements to be finalized. No one wanted to be in the back, and everyone wanted to be near the witch, if not directly next to her. People of all kinds filled the seats, each anxious for things to get started. The beastly races were there, too, mixed in with all the rest. Krekatin, the witch's old assistant, sat to her right, and to her left was Tumon.

"Welcome everyone," said Honey. "I brought cake for everyone, it's made of compromise."

No one moved.

"Well I'm going to try some." Honey took a nearby knife and cut a small slice out of the massive cake. Taking a bite out of the cake, her body went stiff. Wincing, she swallowed.

"How is it?" Asked Krekatin.

"Bitter and unsatisfying. Maybe we should just get started. Settle in everyone, I think this is going to take a while. We'll start with the big issues, then split into groups for more regional problems. No one gets to leave, until we've solved world peace and world hunger."

Post Epilogue

It'd been some twenty years since Alteem returned home. He'd heard rumors and whispers of Honey's activity. War had been stopped, at least in the region he'd left her. The world was a large place, and she couldn't get to all of it in time. She traveled across the globe, and where ever there was war, it stopped. Eventually word spread and she didn't need to go to each place anymore. A great congress had been called. Over several months they debated, and argued. Borders were drawn, and a declaration of universal human rights was made. A list of laws that all countries were bound to abide by.

Mathew still visited from time to time, but not as much as he once had. One morning, Alteem left the home that had felt very empty ever since his return, and walked up a hill to were a gravestone stood. A bouquet of flowers rested next to the grave. At first Alteem believed Mathew had set it there, but he'd been away for a few months. Getting closer, he noticed they looked as if one had been taken from every part of the globe, a purple ribbon intertwining among them. A note was attached to them. Picking it up, he read it:

One from all the places you never got to see.

For a brief moment Alteem believed Honey had left them, then he read the next line.

*I never got to meet you, but I heard you were the most
wonderful person to ever live.*

Alteem looked around, wondering who might have left them. He might have thought they'd been left here by mistake, but Alma's grave stood alone. After paying his normal respects to the site, he returned home.

Someone stood peering into the windows of his home. For a single moment, he thought it was Honey, but she had dark hair. It seemed today was just a day for Alteem's perception to play tricks on him. Her body was much like Honey's, just as tiny and impossibly beautiful. Her skin was dark, too, not pale like the witch's, closer to Alma's and Mathew's.

"Excuse me," said Alteem.

She jumped, and moved away from the window. Seeing her face stunned Alteem. She looked much like Alma, only younger and with the same sense of impossible beauty Honey had had. Then there was her eyes, green, only with one a slightly dark shade than the other. "Sorry, I wasn't spying," She said. "I knocked and no one was there, and I've been on this long journey, and I finally got here and no one answered and all I could think was I came all this way and was waiting for this moment, and then no one's here, so I thought maybe they're asleep, or it's been so long maybe he doesn't live here anymore, or worse maybe he's dead, then what would I do." She paused to breathe. "Are you...are you him?"

Alteem didn't answer right away, he was stunned at first by the girl's appearance, then by her barrage of words. "Am I who?"

"Alteem."

"Yes, who are-"

"Wow, it's really you, you look different than I thought you would. Oh, I'm so happy I found you, I was worried you might have moved on, and then where would I go to find my father, not that I didn't want to meet you too, mother's told me so much about you, but I really wanted to meet my dad. Mom always said we'd visit when we had the time, but there's always another world crisis, and we're off to stop a war or a natural disaster and before you know it all this time has passed and I'm adult and I realize, I can go on my own now."

"Please, slow down."

"Sorry. I can ramble a bit, when I get nervous. I'm working on it."

"What's your name?"

"Alma," she said. "I was named after grandma."